The Humboldt Effect

Also by Delia Huddy
TIME PIPER

Delia Huddy

The Humboldt Effect

Greenwillow Books
New York

for Julia

Copyright © 1982 by Delia Huddy
First published in Great Britain
by Julia MacRae Books

All rights reserved. No part of this book
may be reproduced or utilized in any form
or by any means, electronic or mechanical,
including photocopying, recording or by any
information storage and retrieval system,
without permission in writing from the Publisher,
Greenwillow Books, a division of
William Morrow & Company Inc.,
105 Madison Avenue, New York, N.Y. 10016.

Printed in the United States of America
First American Edition
10 9 8 7 6 5 4 3 2 1

Library of Congress Cataloging in Publication Data

Huddy, Delia.
The Humboldt effect.
Summary: An experiment with Tom Humboldt's time
machine from a submarine in the Mediterranean
has cataclysmic results when a team member is
lost at sea and a man from the fourth century
B.C. is taken on board.
[1. Science fiction.
2. Space and time—Fiction]   I. Title
PZ7.H864Hu   1982   [Fic]   82-9212
ISBN 0-688-01526-3   AACR2

Contents

PART ONE

Chapter 1

December

"There's a leper waving to you," Rosie, his sister, said.

Their mother, trying to unwedge an umbrella from where it had rolled beneath the leg of a chair, raised her head with a startled jerk. "A leper?"

"Waving at Luke . . ."

Luke was caught in the middle of an enormous yawn, lunch-hour chamber music not being his line of country. He swallowed quickly. "What sort of a leper?"

"A female one." Rosie's eyes widened. "She's coming across."

Luke turned and, seeing who it was, rose to his feet in a great hurry and with a startled exclamation. His chair tipped backwards onto a lady behind, who received his hurried apology with ill-concealed annoyance.

Mrs Crantock, aware of her son's impropriety, murmured, "Oh Luke!" and hoped that they were not all going to be hugely embarrassed.

In a totally ungenteel world, this lunch-time bevy of ladies in hats and gloves, listening to baroque music in a small DDC studio in Knightsbridge, maintained an impressive air of gentility. A Radio Three recital, recorded before an invited audience. Luke (who was uninvited) was the only male in sight under the age of three score years and ten. The chatter was soft; the applause had been enthusiastic but discreet.

"Mary!"

"Luke, darling!"

If the greeting jolted Luke's mother, it was nothing to the shock

9

of seeing the girl's face at close quarters. Mrs Crantock feared the worst.

Her complexion suggested total exposure to a burning tropical sun. It was red and raw. What was more, it was covered by an angry rash.

She wore black jeans, very tight, tucked into high black knee boots and a tight fitting fur jacket. A vivid pink and orange scarf was wound round her head like a turban, beneath which her fair hair fell to her shoulders, straight as a plumb line. On top of it all she wore a large floppy-brimmed black hat. In their muted surroundings, her appearance could not have been more abrasive if heralded by a roll of drums. The lady behind the Crantocks stared with distasteful fascination.

Mary said, "I didn't know you were in London, Luke..."

"Only for a day." Luke's own colour had heightened. She had caught him so unaware. It embarrassed him to be here with his mother and sister in a place that was essentially not his world.

Mary seemed not to have noticed anything amiss. She had greeted him with great eagerness but at his words, her face fell as if a hope had been dashed.

Luke would have thought of Mary as the last person to seek help. But now as she caught and held his glance, he felt he detected a definite plea.

He said, "I've driven my mother up from Gloucestershire. Her annual Christmas shopping and recitaling trip ... she doesn't like driving in London." He gestured. "Mother. This is Mary Talbot ... and Rosie, my sister."

Mrs Crantock inclined her head and Rosie gave a cheerful wave. Rosie had been experimenting in the cosmetics department of one of the stores and each nail was brightly lacquered in a different colour.

"Mary's at the Institute. A friend of Arthur's."

"How do you do."

Mary did not offer her hand for which Mrs Crantock was thankful. One never knew with *skin*. Mrs Crantock had met very few of Luke's friends; he had always been close about his affairs. In order to build up any picture of his life away from home, she had to piece together bits of information he dropped inadvertently. She had heard of Arthur – and formed her own image of a north country boy, brusque and unrefined. The image did not fit at all with the girl standing in front of them whose voice was cultured to the point of affectation.

"Would you have just an hour ... there's something ... I'd very much like to talk."

Luke hesitated briefly and then said, "Why not? Concert over. Rosie having her hair done. There's no need for me to be around." He turned to his mother. "I'll meet you again later."

Mrs Crantock was not overjoyed. Had the girl seen a doctor? Should Luke go off with her just like that, without knowing? But Luke was hardly of an age when he would take her advice – his present tone of voice was warning enough. She said reluctantly, not wanting to appear brusque, "All right, dear. Where shall we meet?"

"In a couple of hours. At the car. Can you find your way there ... "

Mary Talbot might at least say *something*; give some explanation, thought Mrs Crantock. But she seemed disinclined to make conversation. She stared anxiously at Luke, tapping her foot in a certain agitation. Why did she want to see Luke anyway? A couple of hours was hardly a chat – more like a whole psychiatrist's session.

Suddenly, as if realising that she had created a situation, Mary pulled herself up. "Luke! Are you sure it doesn't upset your plans? Mess up your mother?" She looked at Mrs Crantock briefly, questioning. "Look! I was supposed to meet my Aunt Jennifer here but she doesn't seem to have turned up. I'd better just make sure she isn't around; I'll see you outside by the stairs in ten minutes ... "

"What *is* wrong with your face?" said Rosie.

"Rosie!" Mrs Crantock was scandalised by such a breach of good manners. However much she, herself, wanted to know, she would never dream of asking such a question.

Mary's hand went up to her face, vaguely, as if hardly aware of it. "Oh! *Marriage fever* ... you might call it, I suppose. Not

11

contagious as far as I know . . . " She gave an airy little gesture of farewell which embraced them all, before making her way across the room, quite oblivious of the curious glances cast her way.

Rosie said, *"Darling!* What in the world is marriage fever?"

Luke's face was like a poker. "I've really no idea."

"You do have some interesting friends, Luke. Why do you keep them secret . . . especially someone so *close. . ."*

"She calls everyone darling, if that's what you mean. It's just her way." Luke, impatient to get away, went on equably, "See you later then. You can get coffee here, you know, if you want it. Downstairs."

"I think the sooner we make a dignified exit, the better . . . "

"You're so self-conscious, Ma . . . who's interested in us . . . "

Luke left them, Rosie arguing loudly, her mother remonstrating softly and discreetly as she gathered together various carrier bags, trophies of a morning's shopping. He made for the stairs.

Mary was there already. Her agitation had increased. She caught hold of his arm.

"No Aunt Jennifer then," he said. "Sorry to keep you waiting."

"You haven't been anything like ten minutes. Oh Luke! It's got a whole lot worse since I came out this morning."

"Your face . . . ?" he said, scrutinising her. She did look awful.

"I've just been into the loo . . . it's horrific! No wonder your sister remarked . . . "

"Rosie thought it was leprosy . . . " He didn't know whether Mary was ready to make a joke of her affliction. He found she was not.

"Leprosy! Let's get out of here before people take fright . . . "

"Marriage fever?" he said, wanting to be enlightened. "Who are you married to, then?"

"I'm not," Mary clutched him again. "Not yet. Oh Luke, that's the trouble. It's Arthur. I don't know whether to marry him or not. When I saw you in that recital . . . I was so relieved . . . *you've got to tell me what to do."*

Luke was so taken aback by the total unexpectedness of all this, that for the moment he just stared in blank astonishment. If she had asked him whether she should take up an offer of a trip to the moon or go into partnership with a racehorse owner, he would have felt more qualified to advise her.

Out of sheer surprise, he began to laugh.

He realised his mistake at once. Her face crumpled in a way he would not have imagined possible in someone so outwardly sophisticated. Her eyes, unusually dark for a person with such a fair skin, were full of hurt. He looked hurriedly away.

"I didn't think you would find it funny."

The laughter died in his throat. "I don't . . . not really."

"Why are you laughing then?" she cried.

"You've taken me by surprise. It's just the thought of me . . . giving advice on that sort of thing . . . knowing nothing about it." They were down the stairs now and crossing a big tiled entrance hall. He didn't know what to say, how to tackle the situation. Luke was not a person who found talking easy, even to people he knew well. And he had never been close to Mary. On top of that, the thought of Mary *marrying* Arthur threw him completely.

"People know," he said helplessly, "if they really want to . . . surely . . ."

"But *I* don't . . ."

"And they don't come out in rashes."

"But they *do* . . . I *have* . . ."

"Then you can't want to marry him . . . really . . . right deep down." Was he talking utter rubbish or did it make sense? Luke was appalled to see tears running down her cheeks. His logic melted into nothing before her distress.

They were out in the street now and the wind hit them. It shrieked up the Brompton Road, icy cold from the west. A flock of seagulls came screaming with it, high over the roofs of the buildings opposite. Even above the noise of the traffic you could hear their sharp cries.

Mary was sniffing back her tears and shivering violently. She wrapped her skinny coat round her chest and grabbed her hat as the wind tried to snatch it.

13

"Would you rather stay inside . . . ?"

"No . . . no."

Given no choice, he guided her down the pavement, not knowing where they were going. The heavy traffic parted briefly at a crossing and they went over.

Two years before, he had come up to London to work for six months at the *L'Institut pour la Promotion en Physique Européen* before going up to Cambridge. It was there he had met Arthur and Mary. Mary had been in the same laboratory as he was himself. All three of them had been part of a team involved in research on Humboldt's Time Machine.

At a time when Luke was taking his first plunge into the world at large – a world very different from the protected atmosphere of school and home – Arthur had been his friend not only in the Institute lab but also sharing his digs. Arthur had been the rock on which Luke relied – solid, matter of fact, take-it-or-leave-it Arthur, always the same.

When Arthur had started going round with Mary Talbot, Luke, who didn't like her, found it hard to understand. Mary seemed Arthur's opposite in every way; lightweight, artificial, out to make an impression with her drawling voice and effusiveness that to Luke seemed totally lacking in sincerity and merely made him ill at ease. She was different from other people at the Institute. Where most of them shared rooms or lived in bed sitters, Mary, only child of well-to-do parents, had her own flat in Kensington; where others travelled by public transport or owned, at the best, a beat-up mini, Mary had collected a sports car for her twenty-first.

Oh she was beautiful, Luke granted Arthur that – if you liked the Rossetti-type of classical beauty. And she was intelligent . . . or she would not have been one of Humboldt's team.

Over the summer, Luke had got to know her better and his dislike had waned. She had been kind to him when he was in an emotional state himself. And he found that under her pose, she was more genuine than she seemed on slight acquaintance.

But to have her – the most self-possessed of creatures – asking him for advice on a matter like this seemed utterly ludicrous and

14

he could only suppose it to be one of her deliberate gestures for attention.

Marriage. It had hardly loomed on Luke's horizon yet. People at college had affairs; some short-lived and passionate; others lengthy. People shared flats; lived with each other, but no one in his circle of friends had embarked upon marriage as such.

In utter confusion and not knowing at all how to deal with the situation, he walked along beside her, his hands stuck in the pockets of his great coat. The raw weather chafed her rash and made it look more red and angry than ever.

She burst out, "I can't make the decision. I can't make up my mind, don't you see. It's when I'm logical. When I'm away from him. You must realise, Luke, that on the surface, Arthur is different from me in every way."

It was so exactly what Luke thought himself that he said nothing. It would have been hypocritical to deny it.

Now she had got going, Mary seemed unable to stop.

"You don't think I didn't know, Luke, what people at the Institute said . . . '*God! Those two oddballs!*' Twenty-four hours they gave our little liaison. '*Mary and Arthur!*' I liked doing things like that in those days – surprising people – shocking them. When Arthur started following me round at that party – do you remember, Luke, I think it was about the first time I spoke to you? – I thought it was rather fun to encourage him. I thought he was so *grotty.* Well, he was in those days, wasn't he? Really ghastly and gauche . . ."

"He still is," Luke said abruptly. "People don't change. Only you've got used to him."

"Well, it all seemed a lark. I was getting awfully bored with the glamorous types that lobbed up at home – they were so predictable . . . and then suddenly when I thought it was time the joke ended, it wasn't funny any more. I found I was getting to know him. And he wasn't ghastly – or perhaps maybe in appearance. But underneath he was unlike anyone I had ever known. And I couldn't just drop him like that. We went on all summer; getting to know each other. And he became totally special. *Arthur.* Not just someone I was having a good time

15

with ... even then I didn't realise the extent ... the depth of my feelings..." She faltered into silence.

Luke remembered that first party as if it had been yesterday. When she mentioned it, he felt an upsurge of annoyance that she should have started out with such mickey-taking intentions towards Arthur. Well, she had reaped her reward – got herself embroiled in something more than she had bargained for. At the same time her openness, the exposure of her feelings confused Luke. He felt a prick of remorse; how could he judge her harshly when she looked like that.

A flurry of snow came hurtling down the wind. It stung Luke's face. It must have cut her raw flesh like a knife. He pulled up.

"Look! What are we making for ... this is madness."

"I'm meeting Arthur at the Natural History Museum, just along here ... "

"Today?"

"Four o'clock. I've got to have made up my mind by then. Give a decision. Arthur says we must come to the end of impermanence. Our relationship can't go any further unless we know it's for ever. He's hopelessly old fashioned you know; he won't hear of us living together to see if it works."

What a bizarre situation. Aunt Jennifer and a baroque lunch; Natural History and Arthur for tea and be prepared to answer the question when he popped it. Well nobody ever pretended Mary was conventional.

He said sharply, "I don't want to be there." He imagined getting involved in some dramatic emotional scene.

"Don't go," cried Mary with great force of feeling, frozen in mid stride. She tucked her arm quickly into his and propelled him forward. "Arthur won't arrive for hours yet ... don't look so stricken!" She even managed to smile at the look on his face.

The bell of Brompton Oratory began to toll behind them and he found they were walking in time to its beat. Mary and Arthur's knell. He shivered.

Even at this early hour the afternoon was beginning to close in.

"It's getting dark already." She blew her nose fiercely.

"I think it's going to snow, look at those clouds," he said.

"Maybe we'll have a white Christmas."

They stood at the big iron gates of the Natural History Museum. Heavy storm clouds gloomed above the great mottled blue and yellow pile of building. It was several years since Luke had been inside. It still produced in him a feeling of his own complete insignificance.

They went up the curving flight of steps to the front entrance. It was a relief to get out of the wind. Mary handed over her shoulder bag for a cursory search by the attendant. They went into the hall, shaking off the odd flakes of snow that clung to their hair and coats.

They stood for a moment, overawed by the vastness of the great stone entrance hall.

"This brings you down to size."

It was Mary's turn to shiver. "I'm never sure I like this place. There's no protection against eternity. It stares you in the face."

Snakes of schoolchildren, swinging packets of sandwiches in plastic bags, wound their way across the stone floor and gathered in giggling groups round the glass cases. Eternity embarrassed them too. A little old woman with munching jaws shuffled in out of the cold.

"*Geological succession,*" read Luke, scanning the printed word in a glass case near his elbow. "*All organisms are adapted to their environment.*"

"Are you telling me that I can adapt to Arthur?"

"I say, let's go to the Whale Hall. I haven't been there for years," he said like a small eager boy, deliberately avoiding her question.

"Okay." She seemed less tense now. Perhaps if he had failed to give advice, at least he had served some purpose as a listener. They followed a pointing hand. The Whale Hall was always popular; more school parties were pushing and shoving. Teachers were talking quietly and earnestly – "Whales have *baleen* not teeth . . ." The most industrious children made notes; the inattentive perpetually missed the last sentence and tried to catch up. There was a hum of talk and a lot of sh . . shhhh . . . ing.

"Darling! Just look at Stella's sea cow!" Mary really was on a more even keel. "*Lived in shallow water in family parties. Inactive and fearless.* Sounds just the life. Absolutely no problems . . . "

"Ah! That's where you're wrong," he said, reading on. "Such lethargy didn't pay. *Found in 1741. Extinct by 1768. Hunted down by the Russians.*"

"How low," she said, "taking advantage of such an obviously charitable creature . . . "

But it was the Blue Whale that dominated the hall, suspended from the ceiling among a scattering of skeletons of its smaller brethren. It filled the whole place with its immensity. It was impossible to imagine a creature of that size alive. Its ribbed blue underside was mottled with large dashes of white.

"Let's go up into the balcony and look down on him." Luke led the way up a small side staircase. "My goodness, the sky *is* black."

A large part of the ceiling of the Whale Hall being window, one could see the sky outside. A curtain of dark cloud was drawn right across, pressing against the glass, a tattered curtain so black that a trail of industrial smoke blowing across one corner looked snow-white in comparison. Yet as far as they could see there was now neither rain nor snow.

Then came an ominous rumble. They felt as well as heard it; it vibrated in the handrail of the stairs.

"Thunder?"

"In December? . . . but it was *snowing* . . . "

The whale from above looked even bigger. They leaned on the balustrade looking down. It was a colossus. It went on for ever. Its flippers in comparison to its body looked ludicrously small.

"It's horrible," Mary said. "I really don't care for it."

Luke had to agree that the whale had a look of evil about it. Its thick-rimmed bottom lip ran into a small malevolent eye; it had a monstrous jaw, a swollen bulbous throat.

Up on the balcony they were close under the glass roof. The black cloud was doing strange things. It was breaking up. Spiralling. All at once it was lit by a livid yellow light. There was a sharp crack and lightning flashed.

Involuntarily, Mary clutched Luke by the arm. The lightning

had been swift and unexpected . . . Another rumble of thunder came, nearer this time. Once again they felt the vibration in the wooden rail on which they were leaning.

The hum of talk from the little groups of children dotted below intensified. It grew more shrill. Upturned faces stared at the glass roof, a few with curiosity, more with apprehension.

The first flash was followed swiftly by a second and almost immediately by thunder. All at once the storm was directly overhead. The lights in the museum went out. There were startled cries from all round the hall.

For a moment the two upstairs in the balcony were engulfed between sky and whale. The whirling yellow light was every-where. The noise of thunder swallowed them up . . . it rolled round pounding against their eardrums, like a thundering sea . . . and the whale below them rolled too. There was a shriek of wind . . . it was as if something forceful hit them . . .

Mary cried, "Arthur!" a strangled cry. Luke felt her fingers clutching him, pulling him down, down . . .

Then the lights in the hall went on again. Normality was restored. It had all taken place within one short minute. Almost before they were aware of it being upon them, it was over. There was the whale below, bland and immobile; the children with their note-books, looking startled but no more.

But Mary was gasping as if she couldn't breathe. She leaned against the rail with her eyes closed. She put up her hand as if warding something off – still in a state of unknowing. She struck out. She hit Luke. This made her recoil and brought her back to her senses. Slowly she opened her eyes.

She was dazed, utterly bewildered; trembling violently.

"Steady up," Luke said, much perturbed. Had she been affected by some sort of electric charge? "It was a flash of lightning, directly overhead."

The storm was rolling away, grumbling. But Mary still shook. She was drained, overcome by a great weakness as if she had experienced something that Luke could not begin to guess at. She clung on to him as though he afforded her protection and he held her tightly, utterly mystified.

"What was it . . . ?"

"Lightning. Thunder. That's all. Just one of those freak storms – very close overhead," he said.

"No. There was something else. More than that. The sea . . . and the whale. I thought . . . I thought I was. . . ."

But she didn't know what she thought. She couldn't remember. The whole incident now it was over, eluded her – was as insubstantial as a dream which fades instantly on waking. She tried to recapture what she had been through but it had left no clue behind – except for her exhaustion.

She had experienced something; of that Luke had no doubt. "Did you feel hurt – a physical pain? Like a burn . . . shock . . . ?"

"Nothing like that. I wasn't here . . . I was somewhere else. . . ."

"You called out 'Arthur' . . . "

"*Arthur!*"

Without warning, she fainted dead away, slid quietly down into a heap on the floor.

Luke was not of a practical turn of mind; he'd never been a Scout or in the St. John's Ambulance Brigade as a boy. For a moment he thought she was dead. He stood and looked at her and was seized by panic. Then he bent down quickly and knew she was alive for a little pulse beat in her neck. He struggled to lift her, looking round rather desperately for a chair.

An elderly museum official had come upstairs.

"What's up? She all right . . . ? She struck by that flash . . . ? Here . . . here . . . over here."

He was all shuffling action. He found a chair and pushed it over towards Luke. Luke thankfully dumped Mary. She was beginning to stir. He thrust her head down on her knees, he seemed to remember they did that at school when people fainted in assembly.

The old man hovered agitatedly. "Do I get a doctor? Tch . . . tch . . . what a flash . . . like the heavens on fire . . . struck her did it . . . electrified?"

He meant well but Luke found him unnerving; had Mary been electrocuted? What was the treatment for shock?

Suddenly – miraculously – there was Arthur.

He said, "What's up?" and was down on his knees in front of Mary rubbing her hand.

"I think it's just a faint. Thank God you're here."

"She's coming round." Arthur went on rubbing gently.

Mary gave a little groan and lifted her head.

Arthur saw her face and gave a startled exclamation.

"She had that before – that rash . . . "

Mary was opening her eyes again. Gradually she focussed them on Arthur. He was still kneeling in front of her. She put out her arms and leaned on him.

"Darling. Arthur. Are you all right?"

"I might say the same to you," he said. "*I'm* all right, why not? It's you. What are you falling about for?"

"Did I faint?" she said, still dazed. "But Luke was here, not you . . . "

Luke was telling the old man that a doctor wasn't needed and thanking him for his concern. The old man seemed reluctant to be reassured.

"Electrified . . . she might have been . . . "

"I think not . . . she's all right anyway." Luke felt now Arthur had come they could cope together. "Nice of you to help."

Mary said slowly to Arthur, "How did you know we were . . . here . . . "

"Saw you both in the Brompton Road twenty minutes ago. But I couldn't catch you; I got held up at the lights. I thought you must be on your way here . . . I was looking round for you; the Whale Hall seemed as likely a place as any." He got up off his knees. Mary tried to get up too. "Hey! Sit down till you feel okay."

"I'm all right now," she said and the colour was coming back into her face.

Arthur expressed no surprise that Luke was in London, walking down the Brompton Road with Mary. But that was Arthur's way. "Good to see you, Luke, boy."

"And you, Arthur." It must be at least six months since Luke had been up visiting the Institute and had talked to Arthur. There was no indication in Arthur's manner that he had come to the museum for an assignment, the outcome of which was going to determine the course of the rest of his life.

"What's this rash, then?" he said to Mary. "Doesn't improve you."

She said, "Arthur, it's only half past three. Half an hour early. We were going to meet at four, weren't we? But never mind, let's make Luke the first to hear the news . . . "

"What's the news then?" he said, his face absolutely dead-pan. Only his eyes behind his thick-rimmed glasses betrayed him. He kept his eyes very steady on Mary.

"Why, that we're going to be married," she said.

Whatever Mary had gone through in that brief moment of the storm had worked a transformation in her. She was no longer the creature of panic – indecision – that Luke had met earlier; she was completely calm; *tranquil* was how he would now describe her. Luke could almost imagine the redness going out of her face; that the rash was fading before his eyes.

Arthur moved to put his arm across Mary's shoulders. He said, "Ay, that's a good idea," and Luke knew that he grasped Mary to cover the fact that his hand was trembling.

Luke said, flippantly – because irreverence seemed the only way in which to respond, he was so utterly floored by the events of the whole day – "You must be mad to take on Arthur, Mary. But as you're set on this hazardous course, I can only wish you fair winds . . . "

"Cut it out, could you, boy," said Arthur. "You never were a poet and you're doing rather worse than usual."

"Oh well," Luke shrugged, "attraction of opposites is a scientific principle." And he thought how abominably pompous that sounded too. But Mary and Arthur didn't seem interested in listening to wise remarks. They were engrossed only in each other.

Luke supposed he ought to get back to the car and Rosie and his mother who would be flapping if he was late. They faced a long crawl out of London in solid traffic on a day like this.

He felt totally exhausted himself. Not one for showing outward emotion, he found it singularly tiring when other people did.

And inwardly his feelings were still churned up; seeing Arthur had clarified nothing.

A kind of psychic experience or an electric shock? Let's face it, neither filled one with confidence as a basis for making up your mind about getting married. It seemed all too much in keeping with Mary's capriciousness. Would she be Arthur's ruination; blanket his talent? The finest, most truly original physicist of his year, Tom Humboldt had once said of Arthur.

And could he, Luke, have made any difference if he had faced up to Mary and told her straight out that she wasn't the one for Arthur?

The only shred of comfort was that a union so unlikely, so bizarre, must surely be intended by some sort of Fate – and for that reason alone he could have done damn all to stop it.

Chapter 2

April

They were married in April.

Mary and Arthur. Mr and Mrs Arthur Smith they became.

It was surely the vogue-iest wedding of the year, thought Luke. He had never seen so much elegance in one room. Mary's relatives, who had overflowed their side of the church, now flooded into the reception at the grand West End hotel. They bore down in their battalions – shook hands with heavily jewelled fingers, immaculately manicured nails; they dipped into expensive leather handbags; over-powered you with the smell of their perfumes; trapped you with quick effusive chatter. Mary's girl friends – the ones Arthur didn't like – wore fashions that were daring and international. The young men – sons of her father's business colleagues, several of them had tried to date Mary in their time – were smooth and urbane in their morning dress.

Tricia Talbot, mother of the bride, was in the palest pink, hair softly curling round a single feather, cunningly contrived into a hat.

"She's making the best of it, of course," said a voice behind Luke.

"Tricia's always been wonderful at making the best of things . . . " said Tricia's sister, Mary's Aunt Jennifer.

"What else could she do . . . ?"

"Stop them marrying!"

'You can't stop them these days. They just live together anyway."

"My dear Molly, you don't mean . . . "

"No, no Jennifer. I've heard nothing to make me think . . . but

24

you do have to look at the facts. You can't bury your head in the sand and pretend the world is like it used to be . . ."

"Maybe he has a kind heart . . ."

"It has to be *very* kind," Molly said adamantly, looking at Arthur across the width of the reception. She said sadly, "Trish must have been hoping Mary would marry . . . well, something a little more glamorous."

"He's not *obviously* suitable," Jennifer agreed. "But it's brains . . . brains are the fashion now. We're not typical of the times, Molly dear."

Mr Robert Talbot was an impeccable host, greying at the temples but only – as yet – slightly running to fat.

"I blame Bob," said Molly. She was Molly Talbot before she was married, some cousin or other; now Molly Featherstone. "All this education. It may seem impressive at the time but it brings you into contact with such a *variety* of types. Some decidedly odd. He should never have let Mary go to that Institute . . . I mean," her gaze swivelled sideways, "hardly traditional wedding guests . . ."

"Something of a motley," Jennifer admitted with a sigh.

Was Mr. Talbot thinking with regret of the young Adonaii that Mary had brought home in the past – before her Institute days – and then not married? If he was, he did not show it.

The vogue-iest wedding – or the most different?

Would it set a trend? Start a fashion to find the most unlikely bridegroom you could. One that was not *obviously suitable*.

For not even Moss Bros could alter or disguise Arthur; make his tall, round-shouldered figure into anything other than he was – unsmart, spotty, heavily bespectacled. Arthur had had his untidy, curly hair trimmed. It was quite incredibly clean; Luke had never seen it so clean. But he no more fitted into this company than a bear would fit in at a Charity Ball.

Arthur's family stood out too – a mere platoon compared to Mary's army. They kept firmly together, solid, north country, matter of fact. They were very much on their dignity among so many strangers although this grew less with every glass of champagne consumed. The wine flowed liberally. Arthur's father had died several years ago but his mother was there, an uncle or two and four younger sisters who grew a little giggly as time went on.

"That hat cost £170," the youngest informed another. She was spindly and myopic, altogether like Arthur.

"Bet it didn't. No one spends that on a *hat!*"

"It did so. I heard her say."

A hundred and seventy pounds. The eyes of Arthur's middle sister grew round. She saw a hundred and seventy pound notes piled one on top of the other on the patterned carpet of the hotel, reaching up to the plastered Edwardian ceiling.

"You could buy a second-hand colour telly for that," she said breathlessly.

Then there was the 'motley' from the Institute. To which Luke supposed he belonged, if he belonged anywhere, having worked there in a temporary capacity two years before. Tom Humboldt himself was there, young but now well-known Professor of Physics; Simon Standen, Tom's right hand and Arthur's best man; Alan Blériot, head of the lab where Mary (and Luke in his time) had worked; John Kelly (in white jeans) and Peter Martin, the computer team from King's – they'd not miss the chance of a party; Dotty Lowenstein, Odette, Kristof, Becky ... someone called Nick Baines who Luke did not know.

"Why on earth did Arthur let her do this to him?" Luke asked Alan. He had moved out of earshot of the two aunts and seized with relief upon Alan filling his plate and glass at one of the long tables round the edge of the room. Alan, unasked, also piled Luke's plate high.

"Hey – that's enough!" There was a limit to what one could eat even of caviare and smoked salmon. "Couldn't they have gone off and got married on their own – without saying anything?"

"Incredible baloney," said another unknown but obvious member of the Institute, tucking into the caviare with great relish. He had a girlish prettiness and was called Barry Lambert. For some reason, Luke did not warm to him.

"That was the idea at first." Alan took a long sip of champagne.

26

"There *are* good things about this sort of wedding. Mary's mother . . . she thought the traditional thing was necessary. Full regalia."

"Tiaras and medals may be worn."

"She persuaded Mary. Thought she might regret it in later years if she missed out on it now. It's hardly Arthur's style." Alan shrugged expressively.

Was this the shape of things to come, Luke wondered. Would Mary's family dominate the lives of Mr and Mrs Arthur Smith? Swamp Arthur; force him into their mould?

Was this the reason for the feeling of unease that had dogged him since he got up that morning and made him wish the day was over?

But Luke could not see Arthur forced into any mould that was not his own. And Alan said, as if on the same line of thought, "I don't think it's worrying Arthur. He looks fairly switched off to me."

Luke had to agree. Tumult and shouting there might be to please Mary's mother but only too obviously it was passing over Arthur's head. Circulating the guests with Mary (she smiling and talking), Arthur was in a little world of his own.

The reason for Luke's unease lay elsewhere. He wished he could pin it down for its very elusiveness irritated him. There was no good tangible reason why he shouldn't enjoy himself like everyone else.

What of the bride, Mary? For it was her day.

Mary looked utterly, radiantly happy.

("She looks happy enough," said Molly Featherstone. "He must have something we don't suspect, Jennifer. Mary's no fool.")

Mary, for her wedding, had put aside her usual trendy gear and had chosen classical simplicity. She looked more beautiful than Luke had ever seen her. Standing there at the altar, she must have been a sore distraction for any hovering angel.

The ancient clergyman who had married them – some old family friend – had certainly seemed a little distracted. A little mumbling.

Arthur had stood at the altar making his vows with tears running down his face. Sniffling hard in the vestry afterwards and wiping his nose on his sleeve – his mother silently handed him a handkerchief – he said without embarrassment that he had been totally unprepared for Mary all in white. He had never seen her in white before. She had looked so . . . out of this world. It had done something to him. He had gone to pieces.

"Oh darling," said Mary. "I do love you! Who else would have snuffled through the marriage service like that?"

Luke looked round at the throng of people. He had not yet spoken to Mary and Arthur. He had avoided the formal entrance to the reception by slipping in through a side door, not feeling like a public hand shaking, introductions and congratulations. Arthur being fêted by all these people who were utter strangers to him, made Luke feel odd.

"Water ice or french pastry, sir?"

The effect of the caviare having now worn off, Luke rejected the water ice as insubstantial. He had a mouth full of crumbling french pastry when he felt a tap on the arm.

"Luke."

In a voice thickly muffled with cream, he said, "Tom!"

"How are the latest formulae?"

How typical of Tom. He was as out of place at the wedding as Arthur although for a different reason. Tom's mind did not run on things like weddings. It ran exclusively on work – physics and physics experiments. Luke supposed that Tom would not have arrived where he was – Professor at twenty-six – had he not been so totally dedicated.

He had altered little in the couple of years since Luke had first met him at the Institute. His dark hair stood up in a shock off his forehead in just the same way and as he talked quickly and excitedly about his projects, his eyes still stabbed you with the ferocity of his enthusiasm.

"How's Cambridge?" he asked. "Good?"

"Enormously."

"You didn't bring that work with you by any chance . . . ?"

"Well, no." Luke did not think you usually came to a wedding with your pockets stuffed with physics equations. Tom obviously thought you did.

"Pity. Never mind, you can probably remember . . . it's the general principle that matters. Are we going to be able to control the moment in the decelerating process of the tachyon when the jump occurs?"

"I think you are."

Tom gripped Luke's elbow. "You really think so. *I* think so too. Have you got any paper on you?" He looked round and whipped up a Marriage Service sheet that someone had dropped on a chair. "Pencil?" He clapped his pockets, then realised what suit he was wearing and said, "Blast!"

"Water ice, sir, or french pastry . . . ?"

"I'd rather have a pencil."

And nothing being too much trouble, the waiter fetched him one.

Tom sat down at one of the long serving tables and said, "Is this what you worked out . . . ?"

"Smile, sir, smile please."

"What's that idiot on about?" said Tom, glaring.

"He's taking photographs."

"Tell him to push off . . . "

Luke had to laugh. But he turned his own back.

The photographer went off to find more obliging subjects.

"They're about to have the speeches."

Tom gave an exclamation of impatience as if having speeches was not part of the day's work and weddings in general got in the way of more important things. And he scribbled away without a pause through the Uncle-proposing-the-health-of-the-bride-and-groom.

Brigadier Kitchener Cox. Luke caught the name murmured among the guests. He seemed to have a reputation; Luke felt he should have heard of him. He made a good job of Mary. Who wouldn't? Mary was a gift to any speech-maker. (Arthur stood looking at his wife as if he still couldn't believe his good fortune; Mary looked lightly into the middle distance as though the talk was all about someone else.)

But when Brigadier K-C came to Arthur, he was defeated. Arthur's qualities were not likely to appeal to the army, Luke thought, momentarily amused. He was so essentially a non-combatant. The Brigadier would no doubt love to get his hands on Arthur; give him a couple of hours unrelenting square-bashing. He seized upon the Institute and dwelt on that rather than on the bridegroom.

" . . . and we actually have here with us today, the Professor himself, Thomas Humboldt . . . "

Everyone turned round, craning.

"They're talking about you, Tom. Take your bow!"

"Eh?" said Tom, engrossed in his physics figures. Luckily he was sitting below the level of most of the guests and was well screened from view.

Luke changed his weight to his other leg.

The speeches were made from a kind of rostrum at one end of the room; the rostrum was surrounded by flowers – yellow roses and gardenias to match the bouquet carried by Mary. When at last it was all over, the last telegram read by Simon, the wedding party stood pinpointed in soft spot-lighting like a group of actors. Someone thumped Simon on the back; he had been a splendid best man.

Were they acting – acting out a farce? Was Mary's radiance a put-on show? Surely she hadn't that amount of acting talent – to make it appear so completely genuine.

Nevertheless Luke could not throw off his depression.

"Will it work out?"

"It is working out," said Tom, misunderstanding.

"Not the formulae. Mary and Arthur . . . ?"

"Oh." Tom looked up, distant, pre-occupied. "I'd think so. They've known each other for two years and Mary is going on at the Institute – it won't really make all that much difference . . . "

Personal relationships were not Tom's line. Theories but not people.

Would Tom himself ever get married? He would be quite impossible to live with, Luke thought. He couldn't imagine Tom with a wife.

30

"Are these the same as your results, Luke?"

"Heavens. I'm not sure of the figures offhand . . . "

"Here. Sit down . . . I'll show you how I got them."

Mary and Arthur went off to change. They had a plane to catch.

It was all drawing to a close.

Luke felt sour with himself. He had let the day be spoiled by foolish imaginings; no, nothing so well defined as imaginings; a formless neurosis . . .

He concentrated on what Tom was saying about his equations.

When the rest of the Institute people came over ten minutes later, the two of them were deep in discussion. Bits of Marriage Service lay everywhere covered in Tom's minute handwriting.

"Christ! You're not working . . . ?"

Tom didn't even look up. He held up his right hand to silence any interruption while his left hand went on writing, " . . . now taking the co-efficients under the transformation, we get . . . "

Simon Standen was not intimidated. "We're going to see a film, Tom, after this is over. Will you cast your vote as to what . . . "

Humboldt, jubilant, said, "Simon! Luke has come to the same conclusion as I have. The thing is on! I'm sure of it . . . we can have a station abroad and control it from the lab here . . . the possibilities are enormous . . . "

"Oh c'mon, Tom!" Dotty Lowenstein started to gather up the scribbled pieces of paper. Dotty had a small white face that belied her resilience for she was in fact tough and humorous, a brilliant mathematician and no respecter of persons. "You're a real bore. Quit working, for God's sake, and enjoy yourself."

"He *is* enjoying himself . . . "

"Hey!" Tom looked up, annoyed at her high-handed action.

But she was unrepentant. "It's Arthur's wedding day. Remember? We're all going somewhere to celebrate further."

"Haven't we celebrated enough?" Tom said disgruntled. "It isn't as if I get much chance to see Luke these days."

"Don't worry, he's coming too."

"Is he?" Luke said in surprise.

"Of course. You can't just melt away. It's always flat as a pancake when they go off. We must do something . . ."

"They're away!" A cry like a hunting call echoed round the big room. Everyone drifted purposefully towards the door, anxious to see them go. They moved down the gilt stairs to the entrance hall, banked with hydrangeas.

Luke was divided from the bridal couple by a wedge of people. He had still not spoken to either of them all day – entirely his own fault.

Arthur, now in jeans, looked more recognisably himself. (Behind Luke someone lamented that youth these days just didn't seem to enjoy glamour; they shed it as soon as possible.)

Luke found himself next to Arthur's mother.

She said, "You're Luke, aren't you? I've heard of you from Arthur." She gripped his arm. "She's a lovely girl, isn't she, but did he have to choose her – she's not our sort?"

She was very open and genuine; so like Arthur.

He said (and hoped he sounded convincing), "They'll be all right. Don't worry. Arthur isn't the sort to make mistakes."

"You'd better come, Ma. Viv's in the lav being sick." A dishevelled sister wriggled her way through the press of people.

Mrs. Smith clicked her tongue but went off after her without showing surprise.

Mary and Arthur were almost off. They had hired a car to take them to the airport. The sunlight was brilliant in the forecourt of the hotel; a showy day that reflected the tempo of the occasion – flying cloud and wind and patches of sharp dazzling light.

Luke found himself sweating. Why didn't they hurry up and go? People were delaying them; throwing confetti, trying to tie shoes on to the bumper of the car. Mary and Arthur were putting up with it all good-humouredly. Arthur had a protective arm round Mary.

Suddenly he wanted to speak to them, shout good luck in an effort to rid himself of this doom feeling. He squeezed between two smart girl friends of Mary's, trod on their toes and got cold looks.

"Oh really . . ."

"Sorry," he said and went on pushing.

They were getting into the car and had their backs to him. They were sitting down. Mary turned to wind down the window and an excited young man thrust confetti at her. She ducked. When she came up again, she saw Luke.

"Good luck," he said loudly. She couldn't possibly know what he was saying but she could see his lips move. It was an inane thing to say anyway. Wholly inadequate. Meaningless. He stood there, fighting some strange emotion. Was it just sentiment or relief that it was over?

Mary was calling to him, "See you when we come back, Luke. We'll come to Cambridge . . . "

Arthur was mopping his brow as the car swept the two of them out of the hotel forecourt and into the busy thoroughfare beyond. Luke thought he waved but he couldn't be sure. Briefly their heads were silhouetted in the back window; there was a break in the traffic. The car turned right and they were gone.

Dotty, at his elbow, said, "Well, that's that. I'd give my eye tooth for a glass of water."

"No doubt there is one, somewhere in the hotel . . . "

"I wouldn't be too sure," she said. "You okay, Luke? You've been looking kind of strained all day . . . "

"Strained?" he said as though she was mad. "How come?"

For now that Mary and Arthur had gone away, man and wife, and it was all over and done with and *inevitable* and Mary had looked so shining the entire day, he could laugh at his gloom. He had an almost physical sensation of shedding something. He felt pounds lighter.

"I don't know," Dotty looked at him perceptively, "you seemed as if you had something on your mind."

Luke eyed her mockingly, "Sometimes I just *think* you're bats, other times I know it. Come on, let's get you this glass of water . . . " Now his gloom had gone, an enormous feeling of exuberance had taken its place.

For what was the point now of telling her of the odd events that had taken place three months ago on the day that Mary and Arthur had become engaged?

Chapter 3

June

There are colleges in Cambridge which are hard to find; Selwyn beyond the Backs or Emmanuel towards Parker's Piece. But you can't miss Caius for it is part of Trinity Street and its chateau-type windows hang over as you walk towards the centre of the town. Statues (of Caius himself and other worthy gentlemen) look down on you from their pedestals as you turn in at the gate.

Arthur and Simon Standen, up for the day from London, turned in here. They crossed Tree Court where the vivid purple flower of a shrub was bursting into colour on the far wall. Arthur nipped a pungent leaf from a line of catmint bushes, crushing it between his fingers and holding it to his nose like snuff. Under the decorative Gate of Virtue they went ("Italianised Gothic," said Simon; he prided himself on knowing something about architecture) and into Caius Court.

"Are his rooms here?"

But they were not. Arthur, who knew them from a previous visit, led the way into a third, smaller court, named after Gonville, co-founder of the College. Luke was Staircase F, rooms on the first floor.

There was no answer to their knock.

"Go in. He's expecting us. He won't be far away."

Simon looked round with interest, never having visited Luke before. A half-finished game of backgammon lay on the low window-sill; there were too many chairs, for Luke had brought two extra from home – Windsor chairs left to him by a great-uncle and much more suited to his college rooms than to his neat, modern bedroom at Grimms in Gloucestershire. On the mantelpiece was a photograph of the Crantock family sprawled on the lawn at home – Luke was built on the lines of his father, tall and spare, Simon noticed.

Invitations were thrust in a wadge behind a grave sandalwood Buddha; there was a sadly fossilised plant, neglected Christmas present from Rosie; notices of rowing activities. A squash racquet stood propped in one corner. Luke's interests seemed ordinary as any young man up at college. A threadbare dressing gown was flung over a chair, Arthur remembered it from three years ago, it had been decrepit then.

And everywhere there were papers. Had Luke been working frantically to get something finished before he went out; a tower of unwashed coffee cups suggested a late night session.

All in all, Simon decided, it didn't look consciously welcoming for visitors. He tried to remember if Luke had been tidy in his digs in London, but failed to recall his room there.

"D'you think he *is* expecting us?"

"I sent a card," said Arthur, "and he wrote back, saying okay. There's that pipe." He picked it up off the record player in the corner. "Doesn't look much used. He could never keep it alight. Wasn't a success. His stage prop, Mary called it."

Simon agreed. It had seemed to him Luke's one bit of affectation and not characteristic.

They lingered, feeling intruders, not wanting to sit down too comfortably. Different if you were expected but Simon had a feeling they were not.

"That's interesting . . ." he stood back and looked at a small unframed picture propped on the lintel of the door into the bedroom. "Very cubist."

"Looks like a bucket of whitewash to me," Arthur said flatly, "thrown from a distance of three feet . . . you know who did it?"

"No," Simon scrutinised it for a signature.

"Griselda. Remember?"

"Good God," said Simon, "that girl. I'd forgotten about her. Is Luke still interested?" For a moment he held in his mind's eye a tiny wisp of a creature with a cloud of red gold hair. "Where is she now?"

"In the States for a year – staying with relatives or something. She had quite a lot of life to catch up on, you might say." Simon grunted and mooched on, cursorily curious. Luke did not come. Arthur leaned against the window, looking out.

A wild figure in tartan trousers leaped down from one of the staircases, ran across the grass and banged on a ground floor window opposite, shouting excitedly to the occupant within.

The window was flung open and a tape recorder blared forth pop. Arthur laughed. The illusion of age-old peace was shattered; the college hadn't entirely escaped the twentieth century. For some reason Arthur was glad.

"How long have we been here?"

"Twenty minutes . . . "

"We'll be catching the train home at this rate."

"Give him a bit longer."

Simon sat down in one of the Windsor chairs and stretched his legs. He leaned forward. "There's your card. I began to wonder whether you *had* written . . . " He frowned. "I say . . . you put *Thursday.*"

"Well . . . ?"

"It's Wednesday today."

"Oh."

There was a heavy pause.

"What do we do now?" Simon was irritated, not unreasonably, by Arthur's inability to sort out the days of the week. "He's obviously out. Maybe for the whole morning. Do we wait here? Or scour Cambridge . . . "

"God knows . . . " Arthur was not unhappy to stand gazing out of the window onto the sunlit court. But it did not accomplish what they had come for.

"I'll ask someone . . . " He felt he owed it to Simon to rectify his mistake. "I'll ask the porter . . . "

"Why the hell should he know where Luke is . . . ?"

But Arthur went out of the room to show willing if nothing else.

He was lucky. Someone was going past in the narrowness of the staircase. It was the young man in the tartan trousers.

"You wouldn't know where Luke Crantock is likely to be . . . ?"

"Why I guess so. What's the day?" The voice was friendly. American.

"Wednesday," said Arthur, getting it right.

"He'll be in the maths lab. Lecturing – or rather supervising – he does it there so he can make use of the teaching aids . . . all morning up to about one o'clock, I think."

"Thanks . . . where's the maths lab?"

But Simon was behind him. "You mean the room called the Arts School? They used to do maths lecturing there – opposite *The Bath*."

"That's right."

"Thanks," said Arthur again.

"You're welcome." The tartan trousers went on up the staircase and turned in at the door above Luke's.

"Well . . . shall we go and listen to his seminar . . . if we want to catch him?" Simon thought that it was more fruitful than sitting in Luke's room until he returned. "I didn't know he was *lecturing*. Can you, before you graduate?"

They threaded their way down the crowded pavement of King's Parade. "I wouldn't put anything past Luke. He's bright, that boy. They've obviously recognised his worth. He took his degree in his second year . . . now he's researching."

"Another Tom in embryo."

"Maybe." Arthur dodged a crowd of bicycles as they crossed the road. But he didn't think that Luke bore much resemblance to Tom in any way except brain power.

They found the right building, inexplicably called the Arts School though used for maths. They crossed the yard and Arthur stood on tiptoe and peered in at the high window to see if Luke was there. They could just see his head at the far end of the room.

They slipped in quietly through the door at the back and eased themselves onto a hard wooden bench. Luke, writing on the blackboard, had his back to them and missed their coming in.

He was supervising a small class of first-year students.

"There is nothing mysterious about tachyons," he was saying, and Simon grimaced quietly to himself as he sat down. He had heard that tale before and, being an economist himself, he could hardly agree. He knew the next hour would tax his brain power. His staying power too, he thought ruefully; Simon was large and bulky and the benches were not built for comfort.

"By now you should all be familiar with the present range of discovered sub-nuclear particles," Luke continued to write on the blackboard as he talked. "Hadrons divide into mesons – containing neutrons and protons – and baryons on the one hand and light leptons containing the electrons on the other."

Luke had always talked fast; he wasn't ideal as a lecturer. You had to concentrate hard to catch what he was saying.

"You should also be familiar with the latest research in sub-particle physics, quarks and SU symetrics. These are the bricks and mortar of matter as we know it."

It might have been Humboldt talking, thought Simon, somewhat sourly.

Luke listed the table of particles on the blackboard, still with his back to his audience; still unaware of the presence of foreign bodies.

He divided the board horizontally with a chalk line; on the left he wrote PARTICLES above it and ANTI-PARTICLES below.

"Corresponding to each particle there is an opposite particle having the same mass but with exactly the opposite charges. These are anti-particles. An interaction between a particle and its anti-particle results in the annihilation of both particles in a big flash of energy. The existence of all these particles has been demonstrated experimentally. They exist and are bound by the known laws of nature. It is shown in the theory of relativity that they can only exist at speeds less than that of light, never equal to or exceeding it."

Luke divided the blackboard again vertically with two bold double lines between which he wrote 'c' the velocity of light, and headed the empty right-hand side of the board, TACHYONS.

"The tachyons are particles which only exist at speeds greater than light."

He was interrupted by one of the students sitting in the front row. "I thought you said nothing could travel faster than light."

38

"I did." Luke ran his hand through his hair; his hair perpetually fell over his face. Simon remembered the characteristic flick of his head as he jerked it back. "That's where the matter stood ten years ago. It took Humboldt's genius to see that relativity and tachyons could be reconciled if each particle was associated with its own individual time charge. The normal particles and anti-particles are associated with normal positive time flowing forwards as we all know it. On the other side we have the tachyons, normal particles as before but this time they are associated with a negative time charge. Time for tachyons flows backwards. So we have, for example, a tachyon proton or super proton, as we now call it, which is a quite ordinary, normal proton except . . ."

Simon began to experience a familiar feeling of rising panic that he always felt at this stage of the argument. Tom had tried once or twice before to explain the tachyon theory but without success; it was always at about this point that his understanding and reality began to part company. Simon had had an important and major part to play in the Time Machine Experiment three years before. But he was not a technical man; he was Public Relations, and as P.R. his job had been to draw together the different departments and see that in the last instant they synchronised. He had proved himself invaluable. He had left to the science team the actual physics behind the experiment.

Simon had been out late the night before; he had caught the train early that morning at Liverpool Street. The room was, if not hot, at least pleasantly stuffy. The figures on the blackboard behind Luke's head began to run together. Simon jerked awake. A moment later the same thing happened again. Arthur, engrossed in Luke's explanations, paid no heed to his sleep-sodden companion. Simon dozed happily through Luke working out the formula governing negative time fields in relation to the speed of light.

He was brought back to life only when Luke dropped the board rubber and, in bending to pick it up, knocked some books off the desk in front. The combined series of claps roused Simon. For a moment he was all at sea but then remembering where he was, he shook his head and focused his eyes with determination on the blackboard.

The speeds greater than light are apparently achieved by superimposing upon the normal speed determination of $\frac{displacement}{time}$ the effect of the negative time field giving the formula $\frac{displacement\ d}{time\ t_c - time\ t_r}$ where time t_c is the time taken to cover the displacement at the velocity of light, and time t_r is the negative time potential of the tachyon.

The energy of the system is given by:

$$\sum_{r=1}^{n} \frac{mc^2}{\sqrt{\frac{\left(\frac{d}{t_c - t_r}\right)^2}{c^2} - 1}}$$

Luke's cramped hand writing was just about as difficult to read as his quick speech was to hear. Simon nodded sagely to himself. Sanskrit would have been as easy for him to translate.

But he caught the name 'Humboldt' and pricked up his ears hopefully. Luke, going on to talk about machinery, was on more familiar ground for Simon.

"Tom Humboldt achieved the first successful experimental demonstration of this effect, now known as the Humboldt Effect, and it was this principle that was developed in his Time Machine."

Somebody asked, "What development of the Time Machine is he working on now?"

Luke paused. "Well..ll.. that's digressing a bit but Humboldt is trying to control the moment when the tachyon makes the jump. His latest experiments with the 400 GEV accelerator at

Batavia show that if we can give the tachyon a sufficiently hard punch of energy by creating a particle/anti-particle annihilation in contact with it, then the tachyon will jump leaving the time charge free. By controlling the energy flux from the annihilation process, we hope to control the moment in the decelerating process when the jump occurs. In other words, we want to make the tachyons jump at a considerable distance from the tachyon generator and create a time reversal at any particular place in the world . . . "

"You can choose *anywhere* and make time run backwards . . . ?"

It was the same eager voice on the front bench.

Simon viewed the students with a jaundiced eye. They were keen and alert, living off every word that Luke uttered. They understood it all right, he thought. Hell! Three years ago, Luke had arrived in London, raw from school, sadly lacking in self-confidence. Now here he was lecturing a hand-picked group of undergrads. Simon felt depressed and out of sorts; it was as though he were looking at the members of a Club from which he was excluded. He pulled his beard moodily.

He was disturbed from his reverie by a small round of applause. He looked up startled. That was most certainly something he had never heard before at any supervision or lecture, come to that. He looked at Arthur with raised eyebrows. Arthur pulled a delighted face. It impressed upon them both the very high regard in which Luke was held here in the temporal physics faculty.

It was only then that Luke saw Arthur and Simon. For someone who had held a seminar with such confidence and authority, he looked extraordinarily sheepish; the colour rose in his cheeks.

"Okay, all finished," he dismissed the class swiftly. The students got to their feet in a leisurely fashion, casting incurious glances at the two at the back. Luke went over to them.

"Good God, Arthur – no wonder I didn't recognise you. Where are your glasses?"

"Contact lenses. Mary's idea of course. Not really me any more, is it? Score to date – one swallowed; one down the plug hole. But I can see superbly when they are actually in my eyes."

"You're a huge success," said Simon, affably enough, though Luke, sensitive that they should have been there, listening, imagined there was an edge to his voice.

"I thought it was tomorrow you were coming? Did you go to my rooms?"

"Arthur has difficulty with the days of the week," said Simon. "Thursday precedes Wednesday on his calendar."

"Sounds like a dangerous doctrine," Luke spoke lightly for there was no doubting the irritation in Simon's voice now. "Might lead you into all kinds of complications. Didn't your mother ever teach you 'Solomon Grundy', Arthur . . . ?"

"I wouldn't have missed your lecture, boy." Arthur was unruffled by Simon's annoyance. He stretched. "I didn't know you were teaching, let alone this kind of stuff. A few points, I wouldn't mind taking up with you . . . "

"It's not proper lecturing . . . just a class of first years who are interested in that line of country and as I am too . . . well, they seem to find it helpful."

"I'm glad." Simon pulled a doleful face. "Just so much double dutch to me."

"I've finished now," Luke said quickly because it looked as if Arthur might be about to make a facetious remark at Simon's expense. "It doesn't matter, Wednesday or Thursday. Good to see you. What news?"

"It's nothing that couldn't be said over the phone," said Arthur. "But it's damned hot in London and Tom said why not go and see the boy and take a day off on the river . . . punting."

"So here we sit in a musty maths lab . . . "

"Point taken." Luke turned back to the front, gathered up his books and said, "What and where do you want to eat?"

They rejected *The Bath* opposite the Arts School because although the smell from the kitchen was appetising, the sun was hot on their heads and it seemed a pity to eat indoors. They made their way down Silver Street to the river and the bridge and sat under a striped umbrella below the weir. Simon with a glass of beer in his hand and the noise of water in his ears seemed more relaxed.

Luke said, "Well, Arthur. How's Mary and married life?" He'd not seen Arthur since the day of the wedding. Moving into a new flat, they hadn't, after all, had time to visit Luke in Cambridge.

Simon murmured, his face to the sun, "Do you have to ask? Looks like a bloody TV Commercial for Instant Happiness . . . "

He was right of course. Anyone could see that marriage did suit Arthur. Satisfaction with life sat on his face like icing on a birthday cake. He oozed contentment.

The sun had brought out other people besides themselves. The boatyard next to the pub was doing a steadily increasing trade. The number of backsides and beer mugs propped on the bridge above them had doubled since they arrived.

Simon said abruptly, "You know what's in the wind, Luke? Tom plans another experiment this summer. A step forward from the last one, as you were telling your class."

"You mean working the Time Machine in London but actually creating a time reversal somewhere else . . . ?"

"That's the big idea."

"Where?"

"In the Mediterranean."

"The Mediterranean?"

"Why not. As good a place as any."

"Well yes," Luke supposed it was. "But in which country? European, I presume, not Middle Eastern . . . "

"He's not planning to fix things up on land."

For a moment Luke thought Simon was talking about inter-planetary travel. Was Humboldt constructing a space station for his next move?

But even Humboldt had not gone so far as that – yet.

"The base is going to be a submarine."

"A submarine!"

"Do you have to repeat *everything* I say?" Simon's irritation returned.

"It's well . . . unexpected . . . "

"I would have thought you were sufficiently used to Tom by now not to be surprised by anything he has in mind."

"I suppose I ought not to be."

"He wants you to be in on it."

"Aren't I in on it?" Luke asked. "I've been working on enough formulae for him over the past six months."

"I don't mean your formulae. I mean your actual presence is requested . . . "

"On the submarine," said Arthur.

"On the submarine!"

"Change your needle."

"Sorry. But . . . my God! Well . . . "

"What are your plans for the summer?" said Simon, taking a long draught of beer. He leaned forward watching the water pile and fret endlessly against the bastions of the bridge. "Will you finish here or will you come back in the autumn to do a doctorate?"

"It's in the air but not finally settled . . . " Luke was still taken aback by the turn of events. During his whole life he had perhaps spent five minutes thinking about submarines – he'd never been particularly interested in the navy. Now – since two minutes ago – they had become, potentially, a large and important part of his existence. Life never ceased to be unpredictable.

"Why does Tom want me there?"

"God knows," said Simon.

You could interpret that as fairly genuine banter.

"He's not going out there himself," Arthur said. "Big boy's staying at home and pushing the buttons this end. Maybe he thinks your brain is needed on the spot."

"Are you two going . . . ?"

"Yes. It will be quite a party . . . "

"I don't know yet whether I shall go or not," Simon said frowning.

"What do you mean, you don't know?" Arthur jerked up in surprise.

"Are you so sure you're all doing the right thing, backing up Tom like this?"

44

There was a moment's startled silence while the two of them looked at him warily. His heavy scowl challenged them to reply, but they held back waiting for him to explain himself.

Simon elbowed himself deeper into his decrepit folding chair and balanced his beer mug precariously on the wooden arm. "Isn't it time someone stood up to Tom? Refused just to follow on blindly with this business? Isn't he getting deeper and deeper into the mire . . . ?"

"Hang on," said Arthur, "what mire?"

Simon snapped, "Oh come on, Arthur, don't pretend to be naive. You can't meddle with time on a three-dimensional level without affecting somebody or something." He threw a crust of sandwich at a waiting duck and without looking at them said, "I mean you could, for instance, alter the course of history – but maybe that's too trivial a possibility to mention."

There was a moment of uneasy silence and then Luke said, carefully, "Sounds like rather an extravagant claim, Simon."

Simon swivelled round now with undisguised anger. "Sci-fi, you mean? Comic strip stuff, eh? Well, one of these days when it's too late, it will cease to be fiction – it will be *life* and *people*. Tom will be jerked out of his theoretic moon dream with a nasty jolt and have to answer for something . . . "

"Haven't we been over all this before?" Arthur said impatiently – unusually so for Arthur. "You think Tom hasn't got a conscience. I think he has. Maybe we'll have to agree to differ. But he's not just high on equations. And it all comes back to the eternal argument. *You can't stop progress.*"

"What a cliché if ever there was one. You can't stop progress," Simon mimicked, and Luke realised that this was no longer a surface thing but a real deep down canker that must have been gnawing away at him for some time. "That's a laugh. Give me one benefit from men landing on the moon – " as neither of the others made a reply, he answered himself " – a great crashing deficit on America's economy and more psychiatric cases when the astronauts found they couldn't adjust back to normal life . . . "

"You're a real cynic, Simon."

"Progress you say confidently. Are you so sure that it's

progress? Maybe it's retrogression; maybe it'll start something we can't stop." He pulled himself out of the chair and turned to glare down at them, lounging in the sun. "How much money are we spending? Millions! Why not channel it into cancer research – or to refugees in the third world countries? You could at least be *sure* that was progress, couldn't you . . . ?"

Luke, staring at the river, was uncomfortably aware that people were turning round at Simon's upraised voice. He wished with all his heart that he would shut up or go away. Simon had always had this ability to turn things sour. The excitement generated by the news of Tom's experiment a few moments ago had now totally evaporated. Here they were bickering over moral issues like a gang of shop stewards. He supposed that if he felt sufficiently convinced that Simon had no argument at all, he would get up and refute him; as it was he felt uncertain and depressed.

But Arthur felt no lack of conviction. He said quietly, "It's the easiest thing in the world, Simon, to slam everything, criticise what we're doing – say we're wasting money. It's much harder to be like Tom and keep your vision intact and your nerve strong in the face of opposition. God knows, there may be a time – not too far distant too – when moon travel and time travel offer the only chance of us surviving. Or does that sound too extravagant? Let's hope, Simon, if it comes about while we're alive, you'll have the grace to step down and give someone else your seat in the rocket."

That was a nasty one. Luke saw with sudden awareness that it had caught Simon where it hurt most; he jerked his sweater off the back of his chair and turned as if to make off with a look of angry scorn. But underneath one could sense his quandary.

Arthur realised too, for he got to his feet fast and said, "Cool it, Simon, don't let's hash up the day. My round this time – who wants more sandwiches?" – he sorted through the change in his pocket – "Anyone?"

Simon hesitated for a moment and then said with a surly shrug, "Okay, if you like. Another of the same." It was an attempt – albeit an ungracious one – to heal the rift.

"We need a critic in our midst," Arthur said equitably. "Keeps our convictions on their toes ... "

"You're so bloody charitable, Arthur," Simon said fretfully but he sat down again. "You get on my nerves. You'd better get me some more cigarettes as well."

Months later, in very different circumstances, Luke was to remember this day, this argument, the three of them sitting in the sun sipping beer by the Silver Street bridge; a perfect day, weatherwise, of which there are not so many in an English summer. Laughter from a punt; the clatter of the rollers by the weir and the endless fuss and bother of the busy water.

For Luke's emotions, sharpened by the challenge of a new project, were in a state of upheaval; feelings bound up with the first Time experiment came flooding back; feelings that had been submerged now for three years; that he had experienced when much younger, greener and raw to the world of physics and life in general.

"I don't mind telling you," said Simon, draining his third glass, "I'm taking it easy so you two had better strip off your shirts and get cracking ... "

Luke was on his feet. "Right," he said obligingly with a feeling of relief. "Up the river to Grantchester or down past Kings? And does punting count as submarine drill ... ?"

PART TWO

Chapter 4

August (i)

They sailed from Gosport on an afternoon in late August with a cold, light breeze blowing and an overcast sky. At least Luke supposed they 'sailed' but on the other hand perhaps a submarine did not sail but did something else. At any rate they had thrown off the fenders and the berthing wires, and the med ladder linking the submarine to the caisson had at last been removed and they were under weigh.

The submarine slowly nosed its way out towards the open sea; four knots and a white wave beginning to curl back from the bows. The sea had a slight swell; it seemed surprisingly empty of craft.

The coast of England retreated, shrank, became totally unimportant (hard to believe that important things would go on happening there). The houses along the shore became dolls' houses and the buildings and sheds of the Submarine School at Gosport were childish bumps on a cardboard backcloth of land. Arthur, wiping the binoculars with a wad of periscope paper, had long since lost sight of Tom, Alan and Mary waving wildly from the dock.

Luke and Arthur were in the conning-tower – known to the crew as the fin – with the Captain and the First Lieutenant whose name was Davis. The Captain was reliably solid, approaching forty at a guess; a man of few words but not unwelcoming and courteous to a fault. He had been marvellously patient and uncomplaining in dealing with the difficulties that had inevitably arisen when they were loading the scientific equipment into the submarine. He had a fresh, undamaged face; the kind of face which belonged to boys whom Luke's old music master at school called 'good lads'. But Luke was not fooled; no one could rise to be Captain of a submarine by being easy going; he must have been through the mill himself and put others through it too in his time. Luke felt nothing but admiration for William Bradley; his responsibility was enormous for there was a crew of over seventy on board the *Artemis* – counting in themselves – and the Captain was answerable for every man's safety.

Events in London a month before having taken an unexpected turn for Luke, he had the responsibilities of the man in charge very much in mind.

A week after Arthur and Simon's visit to Cambridge, he had gone to see Tom in his basement laboratory at the Institute.

"Luke! Good to see you. We can get on now – discussing plans."

Luke was surprised. He had thought that everything would have been settled long before. He said so.

Tom hitched back his chair and said in his abrupt way, "Certain things to clarify."

"Thanks for inviting me to go."

"Glad you wanted to."

They were splendidly formal. But Luke felt there was something in the air. They were circling warily; had Tom some lunatic idea up his sleeve? Luke had got to know Tom fairly well over the time he worked with him in London and a sixth sense told him that Tom was on edge.

"You didn't think I would refuse an invitation like that?"

"No I didn't. But one can't take people for granted. You might have other commitments . . . "

Luke became totally suspicious. When had Tom ever been scrupulous about other people's feelings? He was the most autocratic of dictators. He said what would happen and expected everyone to fall in with his plans whatever else they were doing.

"How many going?"

"Few as possible. Most of the team, myself included, will be operating from London. Small is beautiful as far as the submarine is concerned. Fewer people, less paraphernalia, less complications. We'll go over what there is to do on board and see if you agree, but I'd think a team of ten at the most."

Why should it matter whether Luke agreed or not? Tom fiddled with a rubber; it was unlike him to prevaricate in this manner and a tingling sensation of alarm began in the nape of Luke's neck and started to crawl up his scalp.

"I want you to be in charge out there."

Surprise was complete. It hit Luke so hard he was unable to answer. "You want me . . . " It came out hoarsely so that he had to clear his throat and start again. "You want *me* to be in charge?" very alarmed.

"Why not?" Tom's needle eyes stabbed into him. The tingling in his scalp exploded into a thousand pricking darts.

"Well . . . well . . . I . . . isn't Arthur going out there for one thing? How can I be in charge of Arthur?"

"Quite easily. Arthur is not a leader. He would be the first to agree. He *has* agreed. He has many qualities. Leadership is not one of them."

"I've never led anything. How do you know I can?"

Tom looked at him shrewdly. "I don't know, Luke. But it seems to me you have the potential. You have the best overall grasp of the theory behind it and as we're even more in the dark than we were at the last experiment, we must have someone on the spot who can work things out at great speed if necessary."

"Shan't I be resented? I haven't even worked here at the Institute recently and when I did, I wasn't qualified. I'm still the youngest . . . "

"Age doesn't matter. It has never bothered me."

It wouldn't, Luke wanted to say wryly. Tom had always had complete faith in his own infallibility.

"You've been doing some very competent lecturing, I hear," Tom said.

Arthur and Simon had been talking.

He said then, "Simon! Simon – of course!" Simon was the obvious choice – must be. He saw him like a big truculent Norse god, lying in the punt on the Cam. He didn't relish being in authority over Simon.

But Tom frowned and said, "Simon hasn't got the technical knowledge, Luke. He knows he hasn't and it's beginning to irk him. He'll stay in London here with me if he wants to be in on it at all." He paused and flipped a key in the air and caught it; the problem of Simon bothered Tom; Simon was a very old friend. "He's been so bloody uptight recently. Don't know what's got in to him. It's ridiculous because he's invaluable on his own thing." He shrugged slightly. "But the first consideration is that everything runs smoothly. Simon – moody – on a submarine would be fatal – mass suicide." He looked at Luke very directly. "Do you want to think about it? I can't force it on you. I realise the responsibility it entails. But I wouldn't ask you to do it if I didn't think you were the best man for the job. Last time we were all working from London which meant I could hold everything together myself. Now I must have someone in charge out there who I have absolute faith in. I'm staking my whole reputation on whoever it is. And you're the only person, Luke, I'm prepared to do that with."

Luke felt that he was walking along a narrow ridge with a yawning precipice on either side. If he fell either way the effect would be nasty – and fatal. He had been paid an enormous compliment; possibly the biggest compliment he would ever be paid in his life. But such were his feelings, he could have done without it.

"Can't we work out there as a team . . . under your orders from London?"

It was a forlorn hope.

"In the last resort someone has to be responsible for any decision. You can't possibly foresee what may arise, and hundreds of miles away in the lab here, I might not be in a position to decide for you."

How could he refuse? Luke knew he couldn't. If he did he would never have any pride in his position again; he would know himself for someone who chickened out when the pressure was on. Yet if he agreed . . . he could already anticipate the sleepless nights, the sweat on the palms of his hands as they waited for the

Instant Time Reversal. What if he made some fatal error of judgment? Messed the whole thing up? It didn't bear thinking about.

His feelings towards Tom had always been a mixture of admiration and irritation. Admiration because he was so undeniably first class – and irritation because he was so damnably demanding and invariably got his own way. Perhaps one followed inevitably on the other.

There was a silence in the room. Luke could hear his heart beating; his thoughts ticking over like a clock.

"I don't . . . "

"What . . . ?"

Tom said, "C'mon Luke, don't feel it's worse than it is. You'll have a first-class team working with you."

Typical Tom; he said think it over and then expected you to decide on the spot. Blast him; he knew perfectly well that Luke was going to say yes.

"Well . . . ?"

"You're a louse, Tom."

"Part of my job," said the unrepentant louse.

"Okay. Tell me about it. But, my God, I hope your confidence isn't misplaced."

Tom said cheerfully, "I don't think so." And he went over to the console briskly, humming, and picked up some books in a businesslike way as if Luke's 'yes' now being a thing of the past, it was just one more small detail he could pigeon-hole as solved before the experiment went critical. Luke saw Tom's whole mind as a set of pigeon-holes; his consent was pushed into one marked 'Done with'. He wished he could isolate things so dispassionately; his own problems seemed to overflow and impinge on each other and refuse to be departmentalised . . .

So here he was now on the bridge of the *Artemis* beside the Captain, feeling like a leaf precariously afloat on the current of a river which would drag him under once he became waterlogged; he just had to stay on the surface for as long as he could.

Tom had originally approached the Admiralty with a view to

merely having apparatus shipped abroad. It hadn't crossed his mind to conduct the experiment at sea. But the navy said why not? The *Artemis* would be doing final tests in the Mediterranean prior to being taken out of service; they could find room for a small team of scientists on board if he liked to make use of it.

This bit of vision on the part of the top brass had impressed Tom. When he did consider the sea as a possible operational field it certainly had advantages; an area of isolation free from interference – and with the team on board a protected vessel. That weighed heavily as a consideration; no one knew the effect the test would have on the surrounding area.

Was this a sad occasion for the Captain, Luke wondered? The *Artemis* on her last tour of duty. Built at the end of the Second World War, she had been considered revolutionary in her time. But now her cramped interior and her diesel engines were hopelessly old fashioned and she was to be broken up. Later in the autumn William Bradley was to be given command of one of the new nuclear-powered subs. Another feather in his cap.

Luke could find no trace of emotion in his face as he watched the horizon; the unshakeable calm of the man in charge, he thought wryly. Tom was the same, of course; he never appeared to suffer from any lack of confidence; arrogance some people called it. But Luke was beginning to realise it was an essential part of being top dog. He must learn to cultivate it himself; he was now one of *them*, he thought morosely, with this newly imposed responsibility for the success of the Humboldt Effect.

A gust of wind from the open sea caught him on the side of the cheek and he turned to face it. Well, it had begun. At last. The gnawing anxiety that had hung over him for the last few weeks of planning, the depression and elation that had alternatively taken possession of him, suddenly fell away and he felt nothing but a kind of businesslike freedom from feeling, a calm resolution and a great eagerness to get on with the job at last.

"Do you dive when you feel like it, sir?"

"Not at all. I have a diving course charted for me, on these short trips – 'jollies' we call them. I follow that. We'll do most of the journey to the Mediterranean under the surface." The Captain looked down at the bow of the ship pushing the wall of water before it. He stood easily, his knees flexing to the movement of the submarine; Luke had to hold the bridge casing to keep his balance. "Waste of power. Submarines are designed to be submerged. In a moment when we're clear of the harbour, we shall take her for a trim dive."

Arthur said, "Come again?"

"We dive to check everything in the ship is working – leaving just the snorkel above the surface."

Luke wondered if William Bradley resented Arthur's conversational tone. It was hardly formal. But you wouldn't turn Arthur into a hardened sailor in ten years let alone ten days.

"We'll give you warning so you don't get wet," said Davis.

They smiled politely, remembering that rule No. 1 was to get on with the navy; they feared their politeness might wear thin by the end of the trip – they found Davis more than a little heavy going.

The quiet command from the Captain came ten minutes later.

"Diving stations."

Speakers throughout the ship carried word to every man on board and the alarm on the bridge bellowed the same message. No one was left in doubt.

Leave the bridge and the wind and the sky. Hold tight to every available handle. Luke and Arthur dropped through the hatch into the control room below. Every clip on the hatches was quickly tightened with a wrench. How long would it take to get used to these precipitous ladders? The crew ran up and down like monkeys; Luke still had to feel around for every rung and continually cracked his shoulder blades on the narrow hatchway.

The engine room reported to the control room that it was ready to dive. Fore-ends reported ready. All look-outs reported below. "All main vents clear." The calls came in swift rotation.

The roar of the diesel engines stopped; there was a brief moment of silence before the quiet hum of the electric motors took over. The control room, a mere twelve foot square, seemed crammed with people. Luke stood pressed against the diving officer, a small hawkish man who was keeping his beady eye on the signal board, a pattern of red and green lights, called by those in the know, *the Christmas tree.*

"Green board."

"Air," said William Bradley.

There was a boom of escaping air as the vents on the saddle tanks were opened and the *Artemis* began to tilt forward as the two planesmen sitting in front operated the controls of the hydroplanes.

Put a foot out to brace yourself against the angle.

"Thirty-five feet."

"Thirty-five," repeated Number One, acknowledging the order and passing it on to the planesmen. The needle in the depth gauge creeping slowly round in a clockwise direction had already swung past the twenty foot mark. The hydroplanes, horizontal rudders set forward and aft like fins, altered the depth of the submarine or kept her steady at the depth ordered. The second Cox'n, his eyes on the depth gauge and the bubble in the spirit level, said calmly, "Thirty-five feet, sir."

"Up periscope." The periscope rose at the touch of a lever, its wires making a whistling sound round the sheaves on the deckhead above. It stopped with a dull clunk.

"Like a look?" William Bradley asked, Luke and Luke, suitably impressed by all this routine super-efficiency, said meekly that he would, very much.

Then, "Just one moment, I'll take a fix first."

A couple of bearings were read and the position marked on the chart.

Luke thought, looking round the control room, I'll never sort it all out. What is what. An absolute jungle of valves, wheels, dials, levers . . .

Both Luke, and afterwards Arthur, sweeping the periscope round the horizon, were surprised to find the land had already dropped away right out of sight; a wrinkling grey eiderdown of sea, which could take no colour from the overcast sky, stretched away in every direction.

"We don't exist, boy," said Arthur, moving the periscope

round slowly with his feet while his hand on the lever altered the height. "We're not here any more."

"I beg your pardon?"

But Luke knew exactly what Arthur meant. To all intents and purposes they had dropped out of the world as effectively as if they had never been.

The watch settled down and the crew went off to their quarters. Only the planesmen were left to keep the submarine in a neat and constant trim. On a south-westerly course and a speed of some fourteen knots, they headed away for the Mediterranean. Sixteen twenty by the Admiralty-type clock on the bulkhead, August 23rd.

"Time for a cuppa," said Arthur. "Important not to let our priorities get blown off course in these off-beat surroundings."

For the hundredth time, Luke thanked his lucky stars he had Arthur in the midst of all these strangers. Arthur to remind him it was tea time, for with these soft under-the-sea lights, it was easy enough to forget what part of the day it was. One of the problems as far as Luke could see was that whereas the crew had their routine jobs to perform, the Institute, for the next five days at least, had endless time on their hands; they would all die of crashing boredom if they weren't careful.

"Better check the equipment isn't sloshing around after that dive."

Legs straddled and arms out defensively against the close sides of the passage, they made their way forwards to the torpedo room, a large part of which had been cleared for their use. The torpedo rooms – one fore and one aft – housed more than any other part of the ship, for they were rooms in the real sense and didn't have the disadvantage of a middle passageway which meant the continual to-ing and fro-ing of personnel moving up and down the ship. Round the walls slept a scattering of telegraphists and messmen, with stokers on alternate watches sharing bunks. With the exception of Luke who was sleeping on a separate bunk in the petty officers' quarters, the team were living alongside the equipment.

"Strewth!" Becky said when they arrived and saw the set-up.

"Torpedo men *share* their bunks with thousands of pounds of explosives, d'you know? They must be devoted."

"You must have noticed they *are*," Kristof said gloomily. "Keen boys."

They had noticed. In the battered temporary building where they stayed the previous week at Gosport, they had chance enough to get to know some of the submariners who, without a doubt, looked upon themselves as a race apart from the general run of the navy. They wore their dolphins proudly and the whole place was positively stiff with *esprit de corps*.

"D'you think they were *born* in a cigar tube crammed with machinery? The way they crawl about as if it's their natural habitat . . . eels have nothing on them getting through those damned watertight doors . . . . and the ghastly smell of oil everywhere, they obviously don't even notice it."

"There must be things we can do that they can't . . . "

"Like what?" Becky asked bitterly. "That mate, Davis, he knows twice as much about Jacques Bonnard as I do and the Mark IV super-Pherix experimental scientific reactor at Arles – all old hat to him . . . "

"*Superlubbers*, not submariners," said Dotty with a distinct lack of reverence; and the nickname stuck.

"All looks okay," Arthur said now, pushing against various pieces of piping and glass tubing that were clamped to the temporary console and finding everything firmly fixed.

They had been given a share in the wardroom for their eating and they made their way back there now, making slow progress as they had to squeeze and stand aside continually for people coming in the other direction. It seemed to Luke that the whole crew was in perpetual motion, messmen hurrying to and fro, watches changing, ratings taking messages. Besides which every last nook and cranny in the passages was crammed not only with bits of equipment, tins of oil and spare parts, but also with food – crates and sacks of fruit and vegetables that the one galley – which cooked for all seventy people on board, heaven only knew how – couldn't possibly house. As he hit his head on a sack of potatoes slung from the ceiling like a hammock and scrambled with difficulty through the bulkhead door, jolting his chin on his knee, Luke thought you would be hard put to it to find a more insane way of existing.

The wardroom was designed to take half a dozen people at the most; crowded already with eight scientists, there wasn't much room left for Arthur and Luke to squash in round the diminutive table. They lodged on a bunk in the corner.

Anyway, Luke thought, no one seemed to be minding the squash, they all looked amazingly good humoured. Just at that moment Barry Lambert brought out a tube of Smarties; holding it in one hand, he neatly extracted the lid with his even white teeth, blew it at one of the messmen pouring out tea, tipped the entire contents of the tube down his throat at one go and flipped the empty carton galleywards after the lid. Very neat and provocative.

Of all the members of the team, Barry Lambert was the only one Luke had doubts about. No place for prima donnas, Tom had said but here was Barry the showman, endlessly calling attention to himself by smart bits of repartee, and clever wit. Luke didn't find him amusing.

Neither did Mary. "Mr. Beautiful," she called him (he was). "Ugh! Crude as oil and twice as thick."

But Arthur wouldn't have that. Barry might be a pain in the neck but he was clever and they needed him to lay the helium for the anti-alpha-radiation. "He behaves like he does because he's insecure. Try putting him at his ease."

"Ugh!" Mary had said again. "A real professional stirrer. Look at us now . . . arguing all because of him." She glared at Arthur.

So it was against his will, that Luke had agreed to include Barry on the *Artemis*.

A rubbery, jumpy little man, unmistakably Welsh, pushed his way in to join them for a cup of tea. Greenie Green, he said, bowing and chuckling, Green by name and Greenie by way of being Electrical Officer Forward – some submarine jargon they supposed. He was certainly friendly. Luke suspected that as he had told the team they must get on with the navy, so William

Bradley had told the crew they must be tolerant of the Institute. They would all be inseparable before the trip was over the way this chap was laying on the charm.

"Nothing like a submarine for getting to know people," he was assuring them, "living at close quarters like this. You can keep your formality and routine for those big boats – none of that here. We'll all be reading each other's thoughts by the end of the week . . . "

Too true they would, Luke thought, flinching, all his traumas and panics . . .

But as though to counteract the splendid PR job Greenie Green was doing, a large humpty-dumpty of a face pushed itself round the bulkhead door and bellowed, "Who don't know 'ow to operate the 'eads? Who's left the valve open?" They knew the 'heads' were the lavatories so no one disgraced themselves by asking that. "You leave open the valve and your Engine-room Artificer, alias yours truly, will spend his whole bleeding trip plumbing instead of doing his proper job."

"Don't take any notice of him," Greenie said, jumping hard from one foot to the other. "He thrives on grumbling at us all, does Roly."

"'alf a pint of water a day and no more," bellowed Roly, still only a face, "and sea water for washing."

"We've got some bleeding good news for you, mate," said Barry Lambert. "We all hate washing. We're going to be trendy beardies."

Was Barry taking the mickey? Because if so . . . but the submariner's face showed no more sensitivity than the man in the moon and didn't appear put out. He merely grunted.

"You won't know what to do when we get our nuclear sub, Roly."

"Ruddy Buckingham Palace that'll be," said the Engine-room Artificer with relish. "Washing machines, ice cream machines, coke machines . . . "

"Something will go with the old *Artemis*," said Greenie. "After six years of cramping all that space won't seem right."

"It'll seem plenty of all right to me, mate," Roly spoke with conviction and shut the bulkhead door with an emphatic clunk.

All that space, Luke thought they could certainly do with some of it here. He agreed with Roly on that point. Five days packed in like this before they even started on the experiment. Would he survive?

There was no escape route.

No escape route through the hundreds of thousands of tons of water that lay above and around them. For a moment the walls of the wardroom bulged inwards as though someone was squeezing them outside.

Hey. Steady. What was he thinking about?

He was thinking, without a doubt, that he didn't like it much in the wardroom. Not at all in fact.

A stab of alarm caught him in the stomach. He might be able to disguise his nerves about the running of the experiment but could he keep the requisite stiff upper lip in the face of claustrophobia.

Don't be stupid. Imagine you're sitting in some crowded snack bar off Piccadilly Circus with a plastic-topped table and a juke box going. If you didn't know you'd think you could walk outside and buy an evening paper.

But he did know.

And you couldn't.

The cards were coming out and, squeezing behind Arthur, Luke said he was going to do some reading. He went along to the Petty Officers' mess where he had been allotted a bunk.

Why preferential treatment for him? he had asked, objecting when it was first mooted. But Tom had said, with reason, that he of them all needed a clear head and there was more chance of him snatching a few hours sleep in a cabin of his own. Some cabin. A bunk behind a curtain and a wash basin that folded up into the bulkhead. But he blessed Tom now. Six feet of privacy. The most precious six feet in the whole ship.

He rolled onto the sagging bunk; everyone else, he suspected, had taken first pick. The mattress was like a blooming compost heap; and his mirror sliced you in two with a half-inch-wide crack. However.

He closed his eyes. Let his mind stretch over open spaces – that way lay salvation.

He went back to Cambridge. Roll on the autumn when he would be back there, safe from all this kind of lunacy, and reading for his Ph.D. He cycled leisurely along the Backs, imagined the familiar click of the pedal catching on his bent chainguard. In the late afternoon of a fine day the mist began to rise from the river and the last of the sun was caught mellow amongst the fallen leaves.

He switched to Gloucestershire and the Downs behind his home; he strode along the ridge above Grimms where the view took in three counties – and the dog snapped at his heels and Griselda held his hand when they ran . . .

Griselda?

Was it Griselda's hand that he was holding?

He looked down at it. He had noticed it a lot recently with its long tapering fingers and small dome-shaped nails.

Mary's hand not Griselda's! Mary was with him on the Downs with her straight hair blowing out like a banner in the wind.

Strewth! Was he asleep? Had he been dreaming? But he knew for certain that he had not dropped off, not even for a second. What tricks was his mind playing on him; what was this submarine doing to him that he was coming to dwell on his closest friend's wife? To *fancy* her.

A head came round the curtain. "You okay, Luke? Woken you, have I . . . no need to get up."

But Luke, confused and unhappy for more reasons than one, threw his legs off the narrow bunk and said quickly, "Arthur!"

Arthur came back, questioning.

"I feel . . . horrible . . . claustrophobic."

"You felt claustrophobic before?"

"No . . . oo . o"

"And you didn't last week when we were in dock, fixing things?"

"Nope."

"Then I suggest," said Arthur, eyeing him up and down, "that you don't now. I heard that bulky fellow at Gosport worrying you . . . sowing the jim jam seeds. Telling you how some people can't cope with the small amount of space when they get out to sea. You do look for trouble sometimes, Luke . . . you're just *afraid* you're one of the types he was on about. Well, you don't look like one to me if that's any comfort."

"What utter rubbish you do talk," grumbled Luke, wanting to believe that what Arthur was saying made sense and that what he himself was feeling was totally unsensible. He felt around for his sock with a toe. "What d'you mean? What do claustrophobic types look like?" A great release of tension went out of him.

"Yellow beaks," said Arthur, "and they lay eggs and cry, 'Clau, clau!'"

And half an hour later, Davis completed the cure that Arthur had started. Davis, the Number One, who frankly Luke found a puzzle; an unlikely naval man with his nervous unreliable smile that came and went three times in any one sentence when he was talking to you, and his remarkably broad knowledge of things scientific.

Davis followed Luke into the torpedo room and when Luke said conversationally, "All neat and shipshape" – wishing one could say the same about one's nerves – Davis, looking most earnest and apologetic, made it quite clear that he had not sought out Luke in order to have a polite conversation about trivialities.

"Can you tell me exactly how you're going to achieve matter annihilation in the test area. . . ?"

By the time Luke had finished explaining, his mind and concentration were back on the job in hand; he had totally clicked out of the claustrophobic syndrome and back into the scientific one.

He wasn't bothered again by the walls of the wardroom pulsating.

Chapter 5

August (ii)

Eight hours to go.

Luke felt so taut that if anyone had plucked him, he would have twanged like a guitar string.

"Is the stabiliser okay?"

"D'you know when you last asked me that...?"

"When?"

"Two minutes ago. The answer is yes."

"Sorry."

"You're doing fine, boy," said Arthur placidly. "Relax. It's all perfectly on line."

Relax. Have faith. Humboldt in these circumstances, during this waiting time, was always outwardly relaxed. Luke recalled him in the laboratory three years ago, concentrating intensely but outwardly unworried. Controlling any feeling of strain.

It was fatal to seem to be badgering the team. It wasn't as if he hadn't got confidence in everyone. They were all first-rate. Doing a first-rate job. They were the best.

He must get some sleep. He knew that if he went to his bunk and lay down he wouldn't sleep but he needed rest. That day he'd been on the go non-stop, checking the apparatus, every scrap of metal, every wire, every nut and bolt. But his mind must be clear as crystal, eight hours from now.

The experiment was being run in the early hours of Sunday morning (Greenwich time) when the colossal electricity supply needed in London at the Institute was available from the big South of England power stations. The detailed countdown covering the last twenty-four hours had been carefully prepared at his last meeting with Tom. Dotty was the centre pin of the whole operation, the link between Tom and the new computer in London and Luke in the eastern Mediterranean. And who could possibly have anyone more dependable than Dotty?

But it wouldn't hurt just to *see* her.

He went forward and had to pass the wardroom. The air was thick with the smell of beer. Greenie Green, the WEO, came pushing out, laughing heartily. He bumped into Luke.

He said a jaunty "Sorry, Luke!"

"That bloody WEO – he's taken my watch . . . "

Luke recognised the aggrieved tones of Barry from within.

"You shouldn't have made the bet, friend. Live and learn." Greenie uttered the dictum with a grave shaking of his head and then went off with his bobbing step to the after end of the sub, chuckling.

Was Barry really playing cards at this critical point! Luke, poking his head into the wardroom, found that he was. There were six officers and Barry sitting round the table. Luke felt a great surge of anger, almost uncontrollable in his state of tension. Had they made a real mistake over Barry? Was he utterly unreliable; going to let the whole bally thing down?

He said, controlling himself, "Everything okay, Barry?"

Barry said, "Yeah. Fine. Everything checked, Luke, only I've just lost my watch . . . "

Had he had too much to drink? "You'd better get it back," Luke said evenly, "you may need it to know when you're on call."

Barry looked at him with his beautiful brown eyes; was he mocking Luke? Seeing right in to the whirlpool of his mind? Could he sense the agitation that in a moment would spill right over into panic; come out in a stream of abuse against a member of the team who wasn't pulling his weight?

"Some people find it easy to relax," said a voice behind him. "Aren't they just the lucky ones." It was Nick Baines who was earmarked for logistics. Luke liked Nick as much as he disliked Barry. He was a rangy loose-limbed classic type of American, the kind that one imagined filled the prairies or peopled the Far West in the heyday of the cowboys. He had a relaxed, whimsical air of someone perpetually on the edge of discovering something humorous about life. At the same time he was slightly diffident; a likeable combination.

Nick shook his head. "Wish I could take my mind off things with a game of cards."

Luke swallowed hard and the moment passed. Nick had saved him from making the most awful fool of himself. Of course Barry could be relied on; he wasn't back on duty for a couple of hours yet and as Nick said, he was lucky that he could relax with the officers in the wardroom. Far better than getting worked up into a sweat like he himself seemed to be doing.

"I'm going to lie down for a few hours. Let me know if anything crops up that needs my attention," he said.

"We can cope with most things. Get some rest," said Nick. He put his hand on Luke's shoulder. "Everything is going like clockwork, thanks to you. Well done. You'll need all your faculties full speed ahead all too soon."

Luke nodded, managed to grin at them all and withdrew, vastly comforted by Nick's solidity.

He went on to Dotty. She was sitting at the console they had rigged up forward under the casing in the torpedo room. The linked time check had now been picked up and the countdown was initially being called in quarter hours. In the later stages they would be changing to minutes and seconds. Dotty saw him and raised her eyebrows comically, one after the other; she had a trick of moving them independently. Not for one second did she relax her concentration on what she was doing. When was Kristof due to take over from her? He nearly asked but stopped himself quickly. He smiled and made the thumbs up sign and she blew him a kiss in return. He noticed the mountainous pile of cigarette ends in the ash tray.

He lay on his bunk and sleep did not come, as he knew it wouldn't. But he began to unwind. Extraordinary how somewhere that a week ago had seemed utterly strange and impersonal should now be so much part of him. His bunk space felt like home. He knew just how to angle his legs round the lumps in the mattress so that he could lie comfortably. And he no longer noticed the continuous vibration of the engines in the frame of the bunk or the loud clunk of the watertight door beyond his head when the watch changed. Not even the wireless bleeping woke him once he was asleep nor the billowing out of his curtain every time anyone went by. He had learned to sleep by his watch and not to worry about the light which was never turned off in the mess and which was the same whether he was falling asleep at night or waking in the morning.

His mind ran calmly over the details of the build up ... the anti-bacquerellium had been delivered safely on time by the French air force; Nick had already stabilised the floats and now with help from Becky was due to start the pre-running of the fission and radiation controls. Arthur was back at the console on the bridge and would be there for another two hours before changing with Kristof. There was no need for him to appear upstairs before about five.

What were they doing in London? He knew exactly what they were doing; could name everyone's task almost to the minute when they would be performing it.

Luke had last spoken to Tom that morning when they had counterchecked the final details and engaged the electronic time lock between the London equipment and *Artemis*, a timing link that had to be accurate to the one hundred millionth of a second within which the parameters of the experiment must be controlled.

Tom had been in an off-hand mood, completely untypical. To anyone who did not know otherwise it might have seemed as if he wasn't taking things seriously. But Luke knowing this was not possible could only surmise that he had turned it on in order to lighten his, Luke's, tension. Tom, after all, must have a very good idea of how Luke was feeling.

But Luke found jocularity irritating and wished Tom would drop it. As a consequence he had been abrupt. They were all jumpy at that point. Even Arthur, although he disguised it better than most. Whereas three years before Luke had been so new to it all that he had not recognised the terrific tension in the team, now he sensed it all too well. It was not only the hours they had put in on setting up the equipment on the submarine but all the intense creative thinking that had gone on for months and months before. Pushing back the existing frontiers of knowledge; even an inch in that direction constituted a veritable mountain of thought.

He drifted off to sleep.

He woke at a quarter to five, five minutes before his alarm went off. An odd trick he had picked up from heaven knew where. Perhaps the clock made a little click or something.

His mouth was dry, his nose blocked up, and he had the beginnings of a headache. Even with air conditioning, he didn't seem to acclimatise himself to underwater sleeping. He rolled out of his bunk, pulled out his basin and splashed more water over his face than he usually allowed himself. His head was clearing already now he was on his feet. *Feel good, work good,* he suddenly remembered a saying of his father's; his father who, unlike most people was brisk and on the ball when he got up, always enjoyed shaving in the morning, actually hummed when he wiped his blade dry. The humming got on Luke's nerves if he happened to hear it. Now it struck him as amusing; you got more tolerant of your family as you got older. Extraordinary to think of his father at this point but kind of stabilising too to know that ordinary everyday life was going on somewhere. They had little idea at Grimms what kind of a life he was leading.

He ran his hand over his week-old bristle which was getting impressive. The crack in his mirror enhanced his beard – made it look longer – quite like Tsar Nicholas, he thought. He would no doubt shave it all off before he got back to civilisation; he wasn't at all sure that a beard suited him and it was proving uncommonly itchy.

He scrambled into his jeans, feeling really on top now, head clear, and pulled a thick pullover over his shirt. It wasn't going to be warm at this hour even in this latitude. Thick socks, special heavy shoes they all had to wear on the submarine and he was ready.

His panic had gone. He felt entirely calm; last night's nerves must have been the result of over-tiredness. He could look at his responsibilities over the next few hours with equilibrium. Everything must be running smoothly or they would have come and woken him.

He switched on the stornophone and heard Dotty's steady reliable voice: "One hour 55, 54, 53, 52, 51, one hour 50, 49, 48 . . . " He keyed in his own number so that everyone would know he was on the net. He checked that all sections were on and running. He switched in to audio and picked up Nick giving a run-down on the setting of the anti-fission equipment. Arthur was asking the odd question. Obviously there was some difficulty but it did not seem too serious. It was like a spider's web; one could feel all the little tugs and pulls as the team got going, each thread tied up one with another.

He called Arthur. "How're things?"

"Okay really." Arthur sounded tired. "We had to take up about forty minutes of the relief hour – Nick got trouble on locking his stabiliser for anti-alpha. The problem seemed to be under power on the main cable line but Davis has got a boost for us . . . "

"Good for the Jimmy." After a week, Luke fell quite naturally into the submariners' jargon. My! They were lucky with their superlubbers – one hundred percent behind the Institute and no sign of the resentment that everyone kept anticipating before they started out. "I'll have some breakfast, Arthur, and be with you in ten minutes. Then you can feed and get some coffee inside you. I'll place your order if you like."

"Four sausages and plenty of toms. Tell that lanky chap – he knows what I like. You had some sleep – you sound a whole heap better?"

"Yep."

After he had eaten a piping-hot plateful of bacon and eggs and told Arthur's friend – the tall, lugubrious chef – what was required, he made his way forward to the control room.

The crew there were keeping their usual calm, unhurried work rate, Number One giving the occasional order to keep the submarine on station.

Davis' face was alive with enthusiasm, his smile coming and

71

going rapidly. "Your lucky day, Luke. Calm, sea like a mill pond and forecasts excellent." He swung the periscope in Luke's direction. "Take a look."

Luke grunted his thanks, his mind already pre-occupied with the thousand and one things that had to be done in the right order if there was to be any chance of success. Only the gentlest roll underfoot told him that they were at sea and when he looked quickly through the periscope, he saw the sky full of blazing stars. In this relatively unpolluted zone they seemed ten times brighter than they did in London. He could just make out the dark blue of the shifting waves and the great shadow of the helium canopy. He swung the periscope round and thought he could distinguish the first light of dawn showing faintly in the east.

"Thanks. I'll be off up outside."

Arthur was slumped in a chair on the casing facing the monitor on the bridge. His headphones were slightly forward off his ears so he could pick up the slightest sounds around him.

"Hi," he said without looking up, "everything okay." A statement or a question? It came to the same thing. Everything so far was going as planned.

Even though prepared for the clear night sky, Luke stood for a moment, stunned by the brightness of the Milky Way. Were they really seeking to challenge this kind of thing, the nature of the Universe, on the basis of work done in a laboratory? For a moment he wanted to laugh, the thought of what Tom and Arthur and he himself had been pushing for seemed ludicrous in the face of all this. Then he thought of the number of people working flat out and the amount of money involved which Simon had so much in mind. Were they going to be the biggest joke of the physics world since the flat earth movement? Too late to have second thoughts now. His sense of proportion returned and he said out loud, more to convince himself than anything else. "It must work."

"What?" said Arthur. "We're still seventeen minutes in hand on the countdown and Tom is plus six. They had some trouble on the computer but the self-diagnosis and repair program sorted it out."

"One of these days those damn machines will end up sorting us out . . . "

"You could be right," said Arthur but not looking too worried. "I've suggested that we hold for eleven minutes ITR minus one hour, if we both keep to time from now on. When we're back in step we can pick up the run-in six minutes early."

"How are they feeling about this in London?"

"Tom's happy. Dotty's getting the schedule phases in now. We may have to spread a bit as the helium tanks are being off-loaded and some of the fission material will have to be sealed off but it shouldn't be much sweat."

"You'd better be off or your tomatoes will be sticking to the pan."

Arthur eased off the head set, keyed out of the net and slipped his stornophone into his pocket. He stretched, yawned and raising his hand to Luke said, "See you" and slid away down through the hatch to breakfast.

Luke settled himself in.

The helium balloon lay huge by the side of the *Artemis*. It dwarfed the submarine. There was no light yet in the sky but what there was reflected from the stars, it seemed to attract to its great canopy. The canopy crinkled and rippled in the cold morning wind like some giant, monstrous fungus. If you screwed up your eyes you could just make out the baquerellium canister inside in the centre. The flaps of the door were, at the moment, tied back and two dinghies, one skippered by Graham Burns and one by Barry, were working quietly, going in and out, adjusting equipment on the vast boom that ran round the bottom of the tent, holding it safely to the surface of the sea. My goodness they were lucky that the sea was so calm.

Luke listened intently. On general he could hear all voices on the intercom. It was one of the most difficult tasks of control to listen to everything at once but when you got the trick of it, the identity with the experiment was astounding. After a moment of adjustment, the entire team matched in with the pre-determined pattern in his mind and his instinct sensed the balance of the immediate situation and the direction in which it was heading.

He relaxed and a slight ache in his stomach muscles made him realise how tense he had been. He keyed over to Nick.

"Nick. How's schedule control?"

"Luke!" Nick's voice came back. "Schedules okay – coming in each quarter. We've picked up one or two omissions and put them right. Could have been nasty. We've worked out two revisions both on instrumentation repairs. The packaged replacement unit has saved us there. We rescheduled and with some extra help from H.M.Sub. cut back on time without loss on the critical path. We rescheduled for an eleven minute hold and Dotty's phasing in now. We can take written schedule checks up to one hour before ITR and verbal up to one half hour before. After that if it louses up, they're on their own."

"Well done, Nick. Sounds like you saved us. Make sure you see the show even from downstairs." Luke could sense that confidence was running high. He switched over to the London channel. "Tom! How's it going?"

"Hello Luke." Tom's voice came back as clearly as if he was down below in the control room. "We're all right. What's it like with you? Good you're back on tap."

"All going fine. Lovely dawn but cold out here on the bridge . . . If we cut the eleven minutes at one hour we can run in six minutes early."

"That's all right with us. This new equipment runs much better than that lash-up we had three years ago. Alan's doing a great job running it all here. I'm really redundant now. Wish I could be with you, Luke. . . . Out."

Luke had never heard Tom sound wistful before; it was a new experience.

"Good luck, Luke."

"Thanks, Tom. Out." At that moment Luke felt very strongly the bond between himself and Tom, stronger than he had ever felt it. Was it something to do with shared responsibility? He checked with Dotty that she had rescheduled to drop eleven minutes and then checked his own equipment. He selected a panel test and, circuit by circuit, tested the running, current flow and back-up reserve. The panel lights worked red-green as the checks ran out. A okay. At the end he looked at all the displays. Everything was running well. He heard Dotty calling Nick, "Hold now for six, Nick."

"All right, Dotty. Holding now." He heard Nick start his own count as his operation began to phase out the extra time they had over London.

Luke checked the video recorder. The spent tape looked right for the run so far. He thought at least they would have an accurate record.

"Becky," he called on the stornophone. "How's instrumentation? Are all the videos on and running?"

"Everything's fine, Luke. I've been listening to you winding it all up over the last forty minutes. Thought you'd forgotten me. We had a couple of repair runs. The new fault-finding unit is fabulous and the prepackaged back-up works like a dream. Dotty cut back in without loss. All videos running, constant monitor on that. No hitches. The three on each location have been a big help. Good decision there, Luke. Well worth the extra. I'll keep in touch if we have any problems but none expected. Out."

"Good. Out." Luke thought, she's come up trumps; if anyone in the group was nervous beforehand, it was Becky; but her report on the situation now couldn't have been more clear and precise. She had completely got on top of things. It gave him renewed confidence himself.

"Okay, Nick," he heard Dotty. "Restart five in hand."

"Check," said Nick's voice. "Starting now five in hand."

The patter of conversation and information went steadily on. Time was running out. He rubbed his hands down his jeans. As the tension built-up his stomach responded by turning somersaults.

The light was increasing with every minute. On the eastern horizon a great burgeoning red rose coloured the deep blue of the fading night sky. Graham and Barry working over there on the helium tent must be getting near the end. Everything tied up.

Even as this thought came into his mind, he heard Barry's call for "Red clearance, please, red clearance" a code for everyone else to clear the stornophone.

"*Emergency*. Luke can you hear? We have an accident. Can you hear me?"

"I can hear ..."

"One of the bearing lines has broken. Get the boats out here, quick. The tank broke free and crushed Graham's foot – I don't think it's bad, one of the ring bolts took the main force ..."

"Right," Luke said hurriedly. "Captain. Can you arrange?"

The Captain's voice came back instantly down the pipe. "Number One will do it for you ... Number One."

"Right, sir." They now saw the other side to the Davis enigma – the crisp and efficient naval side that had earned him his stripes as First Lieutenant. "Be out there in a matter of minutes with Doc, sir. Don't move him unless you have to."

Luke cut in, "I'll send Sheila out as replacement. Sheila? You standing by?"

She was.

"Give Dotty any time delay."

"We should be able to keep to schedule if Sheila's here within five minutes. Out."

"Becky. Give Sheila Graham's schedule, last 45 minutes. She can read it on the way across ..."

There was no panic, just swift efficient action. In the background he could hear the Surgeon Lieutenant crossing to the boat with his small grip of emergency equipment and supplies. Sheila came scrambling out of the hatch clutching the helium deployment schedule. Luke knew Sheila least well of anyone in the team. She was a big girl but neat and very smiley. She always wore a plum-coloured track suit – Luke had never seen her in anything else – and white plimsolls. When you wanted her, she was always there, at your elbow, like a jack-in-the-box, smiling. But she never actually said very much. Tom thought a lot of her; Luke sent up a quiet prayer that she knew what she was doing now. She came up the ladder and out on to the casing looking businesslike and confident and still smiling. Luke gave her a reassuring wave. Who needed reassuring, he wondered ironically.

"Barry, give me Graham." He waited. "Graham. Bad luck! What's the damage?"

"Just a bang on the toe," Graham said. But Luke could hear the strain in his voice. "Not too bad but I can't bear any weight on it. Sorry, Luke ... " his voice was full of disappointment.

"Hardly your fault! You've done a good job getting those tanks in place. Get yourself a front seat and watch things and take it easy. Doc's on his way with Sheila to replace you."

"A Sheila's just what I need right now ... "

These New Zealanders, thought Luke. You can't get them down.

The Gemini dinghy had nearly reached Graham; they had been working on the near side, the submarine side of the helium tent when the accident happened.

"Hallo, Dotty. Any hold?"

"Not needed. I think we can keep on time."

"Watch it. Let me know if it reaches fifty."

"Will do."

Luke picked up the count at forty-two minutes and called up Barry. "Trials pending. How does it look?"

Barry came in and began to relay a mass of technical details. The accident hadn't thrown him at all. Everything seemed on line.

Luke picked up the noise of background movement from down below in the submarine; a voice too far behind the stornophone for him to identify said, "Luke Crantock's a pretty cool fish"; a remark not intended for his ears but immensely cheering at this point. At least he wasn't *showing* any nerves. Just as well they couldn't take his blood pressure ...

With a wry smile he continued clearing the build-up to the first anti-alpha fission test.

"Right, Barry. Look forward to test run starting at minus forty minutes precisely." He maintained the general pattern for a couple of minutes and then listened to Barry calling over a stream of data as his instrumentation recorded the build-up of

77

anti-alpha radiation.

"Computer running, data transmission receiving okay," came Dotty's voice.

"Test running well, build on program reading peak. Instruments on plan. No problems. Will maintain peak for three minutes before run down. Cooling good. At least we're not short of water."

Barry continued calling over data as the test ran down again. "Stand by helium for test run-down again."

"Stand by helium for test run at minus thirty-two . . . "

Arthur slid back into his place; full of sausage and tomatoes he looked twice as alert. He said "Ready." The helium test began.

Luke, glad of Arthur's company on the empty casing, listened intently to the density reading. He had never really liked this plan. He had reservations about the concentration obtainable by gaseous infusion even on the calmest day. He lifted his face to the wind. It ruffled his hair but had not increased by any appreciable degree in the last half hour. Unless the density of the helium nuclei reached the experiment threshold level the whole thing would die.

He needn't have worried. The monitoring instruments showed good figures. Barry had turned up trumps on this. He keyed into the computer on the *Artemis* and found that SHAIR and SUPERCAT would soon be running the whole thing. He eased himself back in his chair. It was nearly over now: in no time at all the computer would take it from then on.

"Hello, Tom. We're ready on minus twenty-eight. Will hold for the five to match with you and then go straight into the final run in."

"All going well here," came the report from London. "The two computers are linked nearly one hundred percent now."

"Alan sends his regards," said Tom. "Says how the hell do you always manage a grandstand view, you and Arthur."

Luke said, "Tell him to take a running jump into the Time Field. Second time round he can be here and I'll be in London."

He imagined the scene in the laboratory in Kent Street. He knew the big generators there were building up to maximum power, ready to pour their thousands of jegawatts into the frame ring. The stacks of the cascade multiplier must be almost critical. Tension and rising excitement would be showing on all their faces – Tom's, Alan's . . . Mary's . . .

"Leave the link open now, Tom, so I can hear developments . . . "

The die was cast. Luke had done all he could. He had brought it successfully to the computered control for the last twenty minutes. A great sense of relief spread through him; the tension eased, leaving only the anxiety of watching the hard won theoretical extension of time physics playing itself out against the steel of practical experiment.

Graham was back on board the sub. The pink dawn light had now spread to such an extent that he could pick out quite clearly the floats, cables and wires round the tanks of the boom and no longer needed the artificial lights from the monitor. The helium tent quivered in the quiet morning wind like some grotesque pink marshmallow.

Behind and above him on the bridge, he heard William Bradley speaking down the pipe. "D'you hear me? This is the Captain. Will all service and civilian personnel now go below. The test is starting and we must have clear decks and control stations. No-one, repeat, no-one knows what may happen when the test area goes critical. Only Mr Crantock and Mr Smith and myself may stay above deck at control stations. At ITR minus 15 minutes, Mr Lambert will leave the helium dispersal station and return to the *Artemis*, arriving at ITR minus nine minutes. At ITR minus thirteen minutes Miss Sheila Norton will leave the anti-alpha radiation unit arriving at the *Artemis* at ITR minus seven minutes. All personnel will immediately go below. Please leave the corridors absolutely clear. The watch will be checking that all free movement is not impeded.

"I shall remain on the bridge. The First Lieutenant will be responsible below deck if for any reason I am not available. Mr Baines will be responsible for all civilian personnel if Mr Crantock is not available.

May I wish everyone every success. Good luck."

The hatch in the fin was closed down, shutting out the sound of people moving in the control room below. In the test area, Barry was releasing the helium in a controlled pattern. He unhurriedly checked the monitors, looking for the helium density build up. The meters were flickering, alive, showing an even spread. It was well over threshold level. On the stornophone, Luke could hear Sheila beginning to run up the anti-alpha fission, getting ready for the first irradiation at ITR minus ten minutes. In the background London was talking to Dotty. "Cascade stack . . . over 90 percent and rising . . . "

Sheila closed down all manual operations on the helium station and made her way back to the *Artemis*. A moment earlier Barry had left the test area. Luke heard them arrive and go down the hatch in the stern. He, Arthur and the Captain were the only three outside the submarine.

Morning was now upon them and in the short time that it had taken the dawn to break, much of the colour had dispersed, spread itself out of the sky and the helium tent no longer reflected pink. The whole scene was quite extraordinarily still. Waiting? The sea had the steely look of first light, a pure, clear look ideally suited to scientific research.

Dotty gave the all-clear for radiation and dead on ITR minus ten, the computer triggered action on the radiation unit. The heavy shields rolled away and the control rod began infinitely slowly withdrawing from the fission stacks. The radiation count began to rise.

Down to the last five minutes. Below, everyone was hanging onto the words from the stornophone.

"Luke here, Dotty. Helium above expectation. Anti-alpha good. Well on target. Am watching for a visual now . . . "

"All computer checks good, Luke."

"All sections green."

"All links green."

"All controls green." Alan was making the report now from London.

It was all systems go.

Four minutes. Stacks in London over 99.5 percent rising . . .

Luke scanned the test area. There must be a response. The energy release had to build up sufficiently to force the tachyons to make the Humboldt jump; enough of them there and they would get a power transfer for a big surge – enough to saturate the whole test area with negative.

On the casing in front of him, Arthur's tousled head was silhouetted against the grey sea. Luke had a great urge to call out to him, to ask him if it had all gone wrong. Surely, surely, it should have responded by now ... He tried to control his impatience ... Arthur, Arthur ... what do we do if nothing happens ..? He bit on his desire to shout out loud.

Panic was just beginning to take hold when he saw it.

A brilliant blast of light exploded in the helium tent against the cold dawn. Then another ... and another ... and another. Like great meteors, the flashes came as the alpha and anti-alpha nuclei disintegrated in total annihilation. On the seat in front of him, Arthur might have been turned to stone ... mesmerised.

He grabbed the stornophone. "Dotty. Dotty. We've got visual sighting. It's like November 5th."

"Well done, Luke. Well done! All on stream. London A okay. It's all on the way!"

Luke clicked on to London. He tried to sound calm and matter of fact and failed completely; his voice was high with excitement. "Tom, can you hear me? It's fantastic. Fantastic! The annihilation is really building up. Test area looks like a dozen rockets going off at once. Readings on monitor are good, Tom! We're on!"

Tom's voice came back, at a lower pitch but his own excitement barely concealed. "Everything good here, Luke. Final count-out completing. Two minutes to go. Out now ... "

Luke sat overwhelmed, chastened by its very magnitude. How many times had they all imagined this, seen it in their mind's eye? But anything they could imagine was a home movie size in comparison to this display.

A grating, straining noise broke in on his stupefaction. It came from forward on the casing. The energy cable securing line had chafed through.

"Arthur! Arthur!" Luke yelled in fright. "Can you get it – the rope? If it fouls the hand rail it'll bust everything."

But Arthur had seen it too and moved forward quickly. He clutched hold of the cable and made it safe, securing it round one of the stanchions on the submarine. Luke, ready if necessary to jump to his assistance, breathed again.

The energy release in the test area was so dazzling now they had to shield their eyes against it. It was spreading fast – or was that an illusion? Was the helium tent moving towards them?

The Captain's voice from the bridge shouted down the voice pipe. "Stand by engine room. Prepare to go full speed astern."

Luke shouted too, "Hold it Captain. It can't reach us here, I promise you. Hold on a minute."

He could not over-ride a command from the Captain as he well knew. If Bradley feared for the safety of the submarine, he would immediately remove the ship from what he considered to be a dangerous position.

But he expressed extraordinary confidence in Luke by saying, "Hold it, engine room." The *Artemis* stayed where she was.

Luke rechecked his mental arithmetic. They *must* be all right. He heard the count in London switch to seconds . . . 59, 58, 57, 56 . . .

Dotty said: "All final green links out."

"Final London check 20 seconds. All green now . . . out.

Section 1. Clear and green

Section 2. Clear and green

Section 3. Clear and green

13 . . . 12 . . . 11 . . . 10

Van de Graaff – all stacks at 99.99 percent and rising.

7 . . . 6 . . . 5 . . ."

At 5, all London transmission stopped until the discharge of the cascade multiplier was over.

Luke counted off the last seconds to himself. "4 . . . 3 . . . 2 . . . 1 . . . zero 1 . . . 2 . . ."

London came back on and he imagined he could still hear the reverberation of the searing boom of the cascade multiplier.

He heard Tom's voice again. "Energy of the frame at maximum. Power absorption at maximum. We have it, Luke, but not on the screen. It must be with you . . . "

Luke, looking at the sky, had a strange feeling of tachyons, crowding in from the upper atmosphere, squeezing down in their millions like the layers of an onion, contracting round the earth, crushing him . . . for a moment he could not breathe. Then reason exerting itself, he shook the feeling off.

Tom's voice came again – more urgently. "Luke, have you got it? Have you got it? We have nothing here. It must be with you . . . "

Luke screwed up his eyes at the brilliance in the test area as if by doing so he could make some change take place by sheer will power. Was it a little fainter, the brilliance through the transparency of the helium tent? Were there changes?

He saw a black patch. At first he thought it was his imagination; then he saw another. He heard a shout from Arthur who was still standing forward on the casing, leaning on the rail where he had gone to deal with the rope.

Luke: "Tom, we have it! Power absorption build up. This is it – black spots, more and more of 'em. We have power transfer . . . experiential increase . . . *the Humboldt Effect*. My God!"

Luke ended with a cry. It was as if the whole test area had for an instant frozen solid. Then slowly it began to move again – unwind backwards. The curtain of fire reversed and uncoiled. For a split second there was utter stillness; a void of timeless space as the time link sought its other pole, finding its anchor in time past . . .

The storm filled the test area with shattering force.

The sea rose up to meet a sky of black tearing wind-swept cloud. There was a screaming whine as the helium tent was ripped from its boom; the whole thing was whipped away by the shrieking wind. The silence of the dawn was destroyed by the fearsome noise of storm and raging sea.

The area was blotted out by a lashing curtain of rain and, momentarily, the watchers on the *Artemis* saw nothing but a turbulence of the elements which might have been in any age or time . . . Then the curtain of rain lifted and a great wave rose up, bigger than any previous wave, rearing its head like some prehistoric monster.

And to Luke's horrified fascination there – sucked into the curves of the wave – was a little ship. It was a sailing ship of sorts but no longer sailing, for its square sail was whipping free, ripped clean off its mast and could surely last only for seconds before being torn to shreds . . . He watched, helpless, waiting for a million tons of water to smash the tiny ship to matchwood, pound it to the bottom of this raging turbulence.

But by some miracle, the ship rode the monster, sliding up over its shoulder, out of the curve of its belly. Yet, even as Luke breathed relief, there were cries from men clinging to the side of the boat – they were making no attempt to hold the craft into the wind – and all of a sudden a figure was tossed out, manhandled into the sea. It fluttered like some helpless bird, garments blowing.

It hit the waves with hardly a splash and was gone.

And the wave came on.

Racing out of the test area it hit the submarine which, at its most unstable on the surface, tipped at an angle of forty-five degrees.

Luke, seeing it coming, grabbed the console and somehow managed to stay jammed between it and the handrail as the water swept over him. The *Artemis*, wallowing like a wounded leviathan, righted herself and was once more on an even keel.

"ARTH . . . " But Arthur was no longer on the casing in front of him.

Arthur had gone. Like Luke he had been thrown off balance. Unlike Luke, he had not managed to wedge himself against the console and hang on.

For a moment Luke could not believe his eyes. Then he heard a shout above him and twisted round to see the Captain on the bridge, giving swift orders into the voice pipe.

"D'you hear me? Captain on the bridge. Man overboard. Stand by the engines. Ease forward to the test area, *but don't go in.*"

But driving rain had blotted out the area again and more

swell was running at right angles to the bow, tipping the submarine. Luke, clinging desperately to his console, burned up the sea with his eyes, praying feverishly aloud, *"Save Arthur, please save Arthur . . ."*

The Captain was ordering a call in rotation from the watch.

Port: "Port sir, . . . no sighting."

Stern: "Stern sir, . . . no sighting."

Starboard: "Starboard sir, no sighting . . . "

Could anything, anyone survive in this . . . were they perilously near the area of radiation?

"Steady as she goes. Slow ahead." His own thoughts were echoed in the Captain's orders. Let them cross the barrier of time and God knows, they did so at their peril.

Then came a shout from the starboard watch and to Luke, mindlessly, helplessly clinging on, it was a call from heaven in answer to his gabbled prayer.

"Man on starboard, sir . . ."

The Captain swung his binoculars and picked up the position. "Steady as she goes. Ten points starboard."

"Thirty yards on the starboard bar, sir . . . "

Arthur must have been swept right across by the swell.

"Rescue party at the ready, Number One?"

The forward hatch opened and three members of the crew came out at lightning speed, equipped with ropes and a life belt.

"Twenty yards . . . "

"Ten yards . . . "

"Five . . . "

"Hold it! Stop engines . . . "

There was a scurry of activity in front of him and Luke moved forward to help.

One of the crew was let down the side of the submarine on a rope. He was able to grab the figure in the sea as he was lifted on the top of a wave. It was all Luke could do to keep his own balance. He hung on to the jump wire for grim death. They were in the area of turbulence that was no man's land between the storm and the twentieth-century calm. The crew and the rescued man were pulled on board.

"Thank God, thank God you're safe . . ." The words died in Luke's throat as he stared at the long, crude clothes, the straight black hair and the ravaged face of the rescued man.

It was not Arthur they had pulled from the sea.

Chapter 6

August (iii)

"Take him below," said Luke, numb.

For a few blessed moments, Luke had gone weak with relief. The nightmare had lifted. Arthur had been rescued. When he saw that it was not Arthur, the torture was unbearable. He cried out aloud against it. He felt no gladness that someone else's life had been saved.

Clinging to the end of the hand rail, he went back to his frenzied searching of the sea. He was oblivious of the submariners pulling and supporting the half-drowned man who seemed totally unable to help himself. They propelled him none too gently through the hatch, and took him below.

For two hours the submarine plied backwards and forwards, the watch reporting in strict rotation without a break. The sound of their voices became an entirely mechanical thing hardly penetrating Luke's consciousness.

Until they stopped.

The Captain was standing by him.

"If he had survived, we should have found him by now." The compassion in his eyes as he looked at Luke belied his controlled voice.

"It was my fault," said Luke. "We should have moved back from the test area as you said."

"It was no one's fault," said the Captain. "We all knew the risks involved. Believe me, you cannot afford to blame yourself. Accidents happen at sea."

"We can't give up," said Luke. His voice too was under control but at the same time pleaded desperately. They must search for ever if necessary. It was unthinkable to accept that Arthur was drowned. His brain somehow insisted that if they went on searching then Arthur was still alive.

"If I thought there was the slightest chance, of course I would go on," said William Bradley, "but we have combed every inch of the area; it's impossible that we've missed him if he's on the surface."

It was only too obvious that the Captain saw Arthur waterlogged and lifeless on the sea bed.

The test area had long since disappeared and the sea had been running calm for some time. A loose but tethered piece of instrumentation slid and clattered idly from side to side on the casing behind them as the submarine rolled gently. The morning was still comparatively young; long waves shouldered each other endlessly across the surface of the sea and the green depths by the side of the sub were full of changing light. The whole serene golden world mocked Luke as he looked out to the stretched line of the horizon.

He felt he was going to choke; his chest was unbearably tight and he retched.

Without being wholly aware of what he was doing, he turned and went down into the *Artemis*.

The others were sitting in shocked silence round the table in the wardroom.

Working forward as they had been in the torpedo room they had not immediately known that a man had gone overboard; that he had not been picked up; nor – until some time later – that it was Arthur.

"Is it true?" As one man they willed Luke to say that it wasn't.

"Yes," said Luke.

"Are they still searching? Is there still hope of picking him up?"

"The Captain says there is no longer any hope. The search has been thorough and there's no sign of him anywhere in the area." Luke's voice cracked. He cleared his throat quickly.

Becky started to cry; she cried silently with the tears pouring down her cheeks and she made no move to stop them or wipe them away. No one else moved.

"The experiment was a success," said Graham at last in a toneless voice like some computerised report.

For a moment Luke went dizzy and the whole world tipped. He put out a hand to grab the table. There must be some way that they could undo it all. Why hadn't they listened to Simon? They had been too arrogant. They had never *really* truthfully contemplated failure or disaster as Simon had asked them to. But Simon had been right all the time. And now it wasn't worth it; he wasn't prepared to sacrifice Arthur.

In the nick of time, Luke saved himself from going under. He looked at the empty frightened faces round the table, eyes red-rimmed with exhaustion, the whole team grey with shock. And he remembered he was in charge of them all.

"You're the one to hold it together." He heard Arthur saying it as clearly as if he stood there in the wardroom. If anything needed saving, it was morale *now*; he had to act, not on the technical side of things as Humboldt had foreseen but on the human side before everyone went to pieces.

Drawing upon resources he never knew he possessed, he took a deep breath. He said, "Is everything run down from the experiment? What report has gone back to London?"

Dotty said, "I reported that everything had gone according to plan, all A.1. I didn't know . . . "

"Thank God," said Luke.

"But you've got to tell them . . . ?"

"I've got to think how to do it. There's Mary . . . She musn't know over the intercom just like that."

"Is there any alternative?" said Nick.

"I've got to think," Luke said again.

Nick got to his feet. "I'll go check things over. And report back to you."

Not for the first time on that trip, Luke had reason to be grateful to Nick. He said quietly, "I think it would help you all if you had something to do; go and check up . . . "

They squeezed out round the table.

He stood alone looking at the plastic surfaces of the wardroom and smelling the fuggy, oily smell and he hated it; hated it with all his heart and wanted to get away from it. Surely it was just part of a nightmare? If he could get back to London, he thought, he would find Arthur in the flat – with his irritating imperturbability, his untidiness, his unpunctuality, his staunch friendship. One could accept a death as a result of illness or old age – a natural death. But something so abrupt – so untimely – how could one accept *this*.

Ought he to contact Tom *now* on the intercom, tell him to break it to Mary? What had he done, not only to Arthur, but to Mary too?

He went out to look for the Captain. He was in the control room.

Luke said, "Can I speak to you for a moment, sir?"

"Come to my cabin."

"Is it possible for me to get back to London?"

"It might be difficult but not impossible. May I ask why?"

Luke said, "Arthur was married. I feel I should tell his wife myself."

"Won't someone else break the news to her?"

"My instincts tell me I should. I'm directly responsible. Tom Humboldt – he is a superb scientist – but not so good with people."

The Captain gave him a long look and said, "Won't she have heard it from someone else by the time you get there?"

"No one – as yet – except the personnel on this submarine knows what has happened. I have told the team to withhold it from London for the moment."

"I must report it to the Admiralty," said the Captain, "or there will be questions asked later as to the delay."

"Of course you must do what is expected of you," Luke said at once, "but could you ask them to keep it to themselves until I get back?"

William Bradley moved some papers round on his table. "There's one other thing. The man we picked up."

"I've not given him a thought," admitted Luke. Wasn't anyone picked up by the submariners the navy's responsibility?

"From the bridge I saw where he came from," said the Captain.

"Yes?"

When the Captain remained silent Luke said, "Well?"

"He came out of the Time Field. He was thrown out of the sailing boat."

Luke said, "Oh my God." He raised his hand to his head as if he had had a physical blow. "Oh my God."

There was silence between them. The Captain looked at Luke without reproach. He was a first class naval man. One accepted what happened and tried to solve it. Everything had some kind of solution, one usually found.

"He will have to go back then," said Luke slowly, "if you are sure."

"I think you should go and see him yourself," said the Captain.

"If we have to repeat the experiment," said Luke, "there will be no question but that I have to return to London. It would be essential to talk to Tom."

He went back to the wardroom as a kind of conditioned reflex but the rest of the Institute were still with the apparatus, forward in the bow.

He looked for Davis.

"Where have you put the man you rescued? I'd like to see him."

He was at the back of the submarine, in the torpedo room which corresponded to the one occupied by the Institute in the bow. But here the torpedoes were still in place; long lethal black carrots between the bunks where the submariners slept. Luke squeezed himself through.

A man. He hardly looked like a man when Luke first saw him. He was crouched on the floor in the darkest corner and might have been a pile of colourless cloth dropped carelessly by some untidy member of the crew.

By him sat a rating on an upturned bucket.

"I bin told to watch 'im," he said conversationally. "I reckon 'ee's barmy. Water on the brain I'd think." He smirked not unkindly at his own cleverness. "Too long in the drink."

He was a solid twentieth-century lad from Newcastle, reared on nourishing school dinners and pop music. What would he

91

know about time travel or deprivation or a man who maybe came from way back in time.

Luke, looking at the pile of clothing felt a surge of quite unreasonable anger; was this what they had got in exchange for Arthur? A head detached itself from the garments; slowly and painfully the shoulders stretched up . . . hands. There was a noise not unlike a cat mewing. A groan.

"He's not half bin making a racket. Sort of crying like – chanting mebbe. Hey wailey!" The rating put out a foot and gave him a poke. He seemed a mildly hectoring fellow.

"Don't," said Luke sharply. "Leave him alone."

The man from the sea seemed oblivious to them both. He remained on his knees, the long cloth robe hanging from his shoulders, drying out – although it was still pretty wet in patches and streaked with brine. His straggling locks of hair were matted and dull. It was difficult to see how old he was in that dark corner of the room but Luke got the impression of a sallow rather pitted face which might have been anything between eighteen and forty. As he dropped his arms to his side in an attitude of utter dejection and helplessness, he lifted his face to where heaven would be if he weren't enclosed in the bowels of a submarine. A stream of words fell from his lips, gabbled rapidly. It was quite impossible to tell what language they were in. Some kind of early Arabic or Hebrew at a guess. Where did the man think he was? Or was the rating right – had the experience of being half drowned, of passing through the Time Barrier, unhinged him?

He must be praying, Luke realised suddenly. Calling upon his god fairly frantically for deliverance from this terrifying predicament.

A more pitiful object would be hard to imagine, his whole sagging exterior spelling loss and bewilderment. But even now Luke, his feelings numbed by circumstance, felt no emotion for the man at all. He was there and Arthur was not. The fact that it was the result of their own initiated experiment only hardened Luke's guilt but did nothing to enlarge his sympathy.

He said to the rating, "Aren't they going to change his clothes, give him something to eat?"

"They've had a go," he said with a shrug. "But he don't seem co-operative so they're leaving him for the moment. Mebbe he'll get hungry. Mebbe it's bellyache he's crying from."

Luke turned away. The man presented just one more insuperable problem. How to get him back to his own time. There was no doubt at all in his mind that the Captain was absolutely right; the man had come from the sailing ship in the Time Field.

He had to get help from Tom.

When he had seen William Bradley again he went back to the wardroom. The others had returned there now. As Luke came in they looked up heavily as old men might.

Luke said, "I'm going home to London. There have been further developments – we may have to run through the experiment again." He ignored their stricken faces; their repulsion at the thought only matched his own. But he and the Captain had mutually agreed that for the time being they should not say that the man in the torpedo room had come from another age. They had no wish to add to his discomfort by making him an object of curiosity. However much they might suspect it, no other person had had the Captain's conclusive view from the bridge.

"And also," Luke said, "I must tell Mary." For a moment his mask of control slipped and his dreadful loss showed in his face. "I'm sorry to have to leave you like this but it's unavoidable and I shall be back as soon as possible. A naval helicopter will take me off the *Artemis* – they've managed to get me onto an Israeli Airline flight from Tel Aviv. Dotty – let Tom know I'm on my way back – just say complications have cropped up . . . " He made a rueful grimace which was the best he could do in the way of cheer for them. "Nick will stand in for me while I'm away – if you need to, refer to him."

They accepted at once that if he said so, he must go. They were a group of first-class people, handpicked for their loyalty, for their stability in just such a situation.

They put out their hands to him to show their support. Nick said, "Don't give us a thought, Luke, we'll be okay sticking round here till you get back. Just work it out with Tom."

"And tell Mary that . . . tell her . . . " But Becky couldn't finish the sentence.

"Don't stay away too long, Sir Lancelot."

Barry Lambert's jaunty, insolent remark fell into a veritable pit of silence. Then there was a quick movement and a sharp crack. Barry put a defensive hand to his face. When he took it away there was a bright red mark.

It was Dotty who had struck him. She stood trembling with emotion, anger alive and crackling on her small pinched face.

"You . . . unspeakable . . . "

"It was only meant as a joke," he said sullenly.

"A joke," she spat out at him, "at this sort of time."

"God, you're a bitch," he said.

With drums beating in his ears, Luke turned and went.

Several hours later in a state of total exhaustion he sat in a second-class seat of Israeli Airlines bound for Heathrow, only too glad to do whatever anyone told him. He was incapable of thinking out a single action for himself.

But there was to be no respite. Like a watch that has been overwound yet will not break, he could not stop his thoughts ticking furiously; like St. Catherine he went round and round on his own particular wheel.

For on top of everything else, he now had to question his motives for returning. Was he going back to tell Mary of Arthur's disappearance out of compassion for her? Out of a sense of guilt because with forethought he could have prevented it? Or out of duty? Was it his friendship with Arthur that prompted him – or was it for the reason inferred by Barry Lambert in his foul and untimely remark.

Lancelot, dearest of Arthur's knights, who betrayed him by taking his queen. Did his feelings, which he himself couldn't analyse, sit upon his face for all the world – like Barry Lambert – to see. Or was it just a flippant remark, made on the spur of the moment, a joke in extremely bad taste and no more.

The couple of stiff gins brought to him by a sympathetic stewardess produced a torpor which could hardly be called sleep.

The events of the early morning re-enacted themselves in the guise of a nightmare.

He woke with a start and a cry after barely half an hour, to find himself being curiously regarded by the man next to him. After that not even the gigantic burden of weariness that sat upon him could persuade him to risk shutting his eyes again.

Chapter 7

August (iv)

When he got to the airport in the late afternoon he half expected Tom to have sent a car to meet him but there was no sign of one. He rang the Institute. The cleaner answered the telephone. They had all gone hours before, she said; she believed they had had something big on in the early hours of that very day and she had instructions not to go into the laboratory but only to swill the floor in the hall. They had obviously all gone home before Dotty had got through on the intercom to say Luke was on his way back to London. Did he want the Professor's home telephone number if it was urgent? the cleaner asked; she thought it was on a bit of paper in the office. Oh well, if he'd got it already there was no more she could do for him. Luke rang Tom at home but there was no reply although he let it ring for some time. No doubt he was out cold after the sleepless night. All that speed to get to London and now delay. But his reluctance to tell them such evil news counteracted his irritation.

He set off in the direction of Mary's flat.

He went into Hammersmith and then out on the District line where the train took to the air and flew along at tree top level; the stations along the Chiswick High Road were on stilts and had a quaint countrified air. He thought in a tired, muddled way that London was full of surprises. In the Mediterranean the submarine would be nosing its way north-east.

On the opposite side of the High Road to the station were green squares, pailings round trees and grass; tall pillared Victorian houses suggesting grandeur.

"Not that direction, darling," Mary had said to him the first time he had visited the flat and she had seen which way his gaze was straying. "Off this side of the road. Between the Electric and the Pet Shop."

Barry Lambert had been with them that night.

"Why on earth did you give up your cushy Kensington pad for this?" he had said, eyeing the paint-peeling door as Mary stood in front of it fumbling for her keys.

"We're the Smiths now ... "

"They allow Smiths in Kensington, I daresay."

"We don't want everything handed to us on a plate. The wedding was different, Mother's last fling. Now it's up to us."

"Oh Lord, how very high minded," Barry had said in his jokey voice, "Souls for Smiths. Preferably immortal."

"Why should Arthur live in my old flat with things chosen entirely by me and paid for by my father?" Mary snapped, rising to the bait as Barry had intended she should.

"Most people would jump at it ... Arthur's always been bloody stupid ... "

Luke gave a moan; why did he have to remember conversations like this.

He had been going to plan in the plane how he would break the news to Mary. Now he was on the door step and had thought out nothing. He found he was trembling.

He pushed the door and it was open; he went into the hallway – to name it kindly – a passage rather, dimly lit by a dirty green fanlight. It was drab and sour smelling, littered with advertising leaflets and envelopes addressed to people long since gone away.

"No organised daily, I must do something about it," Mary said every time she came in.

The light seemed to have gone. Luke started to feel his way upstairs. Mary and Arthur's flat was on the fourth floor, right at the top, and there were holes in the carpet to trip you if you weren't wary. He went slowly feeling the wall; passed a yappy dog and the strong smell of someone else's curry.

When he got to the top he was so busy watching his feet that he bumped into the front door. There were voices from inside the flat.

Oh God, thought Luke, are they all with Mary? He sat down on the top stair and tried momentarily to get on top of his shattered feelings. He was afraid he would get through the door and break down. Arthur was everywhere here.

"I'll go," said Gordon Featherstone obligingly – Aunt Molly's husband – when the knock came. Mary was pouring out cups of tea.

"I can't think who will be calling at this time in the afternoon," she said to her Aunt Molly who was sitting on the edge of the sofa. "I'm usually at work at this time of day."

"A rather-the-worse-for-wear-friend of yours," said Gordon Featherstone with a chuckle. He had a laugh like a popping cork.

"*Luke!*"

For one moment Mary stood absolutely rigid, then she said in a great gabble, "Luke, how marvellous to see you. What a marvellous success it all was, so exciting – and an absolute blue print your end. Molly – Gordon – you remember Luke Crantock from our wedding? Molly and Gordon were just passing and dropped in on the offchance I was here because they have never seen the flat – and of course by a miracle I was – "

"Asleep – we woke her up with our knocking, rotters that we are," said Gordon Featherstone, sucking at his pipe and laughing.

"I remember your face," said Aunt Molly, sipping her tea, "you could see more of it on that occasion."

Luke stood in the middle of the sitting room and ran his hand apologetically over his chin. How extraordinary that even under these horrendous circumstances he should be aware of social conventions – Molly Featherstone's condemnation of his unwashed, unshaven face.

"Water's rationed," he mumbled. Then he said, "I've had to come and see Tom about something rather urgent." He didn't look at Mary. "I rang the Institute but he wasn't there nor at his flat, so I called in to see if Mary was at home."

"Like us . . . quite a social afternoon for you, Mary," Gordon

Featherstone lit another match and lipped his pipe.

"Tom's an awful heavy sleeper and he was dead beat ..."

"*You* don't look too wide awake," Gordon said to Luke.

Did the man ever say anything without that idiotic grin on his face. The feeling of unreality was total.

"Luke was on the submarine in the Mediterranean with Arthur ..."

"Ah, water rationing," said Gordon wisely. "Having to rough it a bit. I say, you've got back quickly if you had high jinks only this morning. Did you say the *Mediterranean*? Left Arthur to do the clearing up, eh?"

The awfulness of Gordon Featherstone and Aunt Molly became a kind of fearful blessing because when they went and it could be put off no longer, Mary's face would never look the same again. Let her be free of knowing for as long as possible.

"I must say, Mary," Aunt Molly gave an appraising nod round the room, "you've done quite a lot with this room. When we heard you'd given up your lovely Kensington flat and moved to Chiswick, we did think it was just a bit silly ... your husband's decision, no doubt."

"I did this room up last week. It's a surprise for Arthur. Do you like it, Luke?" She was gabbling again.

"It's very nice," Luke said. He spoke slowly. All of a sudden he had difficulty getting his tongue round words.

"I've painted it green," Mary said. "Arthur's favourite colour ... and the ceiling too, as it's so low ... an attic ... d'you think it's effective?"

"Like being under the sea," said Gordon Featherstone.

She had put some rather arty things in alcoves and got new covers for the armchairs and sofa.

Aunt Molly drained her tea cup and arranged her Liberty silk scarf. "Gordon! We ought to be off; we've got to change before going to the Bertrams." She looked at Luke. "Good-bye." Cleanliness is next to godliness said her eyes.

As Mary showed them out, Luke thought not one word of enquiry about Arthur and all that gabbling ... He found he was still standing in the middle of the floor; he hadn't moved a step since being shown in by Gordon Featherstone.

Mary came back into the sitting room. She closed the door and leaned against it. The look of fear in her eyes was no longer disguised.

"Luke, why have you come . . . ?"

He was for a moment incapable of speech. She came over and caught hold of him by the arm, her fingers digging painfully into his flesh. He put his hand over hers and held it there.

"Luke . . . you're *shaking*."

"Mary," he said.

She sat like a sculpture; like stone, like marble. She hadn't moved for what seemed like hours and hours.

Once Luke said, "Mary," softly but she didn't seem to hear him for nothing moved in response, not even her eyes. She sat against the background of the William Morris pattern of the newly covered sofa, straight-backed, her hands clasped in immobility in her lap.

After a time he became alarmed.

He got up and went to the window. Turned round. Went back to her and sat down on the sofa beside her. "Mary."

This time she turned her head but like a cipher rather than a real person. Someone acting like a person.

"I've got to ring Tom."

She nodded slightly to show she had heard but made no sound.

The phone rang for some time. Tom, newly woken, was brusque.

"What the hell are you doing in London, Luke?"

"I've got to see you. There have been . . . complications."

"What do you mean, complications? It seemed to work miraculously according to schedule."

"Something outside the schedule."

"What on earth are you on about?" Tom, not understanding, sounded angry.

"Arthur."

There was a pause.

"What about Arthur?" Tom's voice was less abrasive, apprehensive.

"He's drowned." Luke who had ultimately kept his voice intact when he told Mary, felt it crack.

There was a long, long silence.

"He can't be," said Tom. "No, no, no."

He went back to the lifeless figure in the sitting room. He squatted in front of her; took her hands. They were lifeless too as if they had no feeling in them. He could pick up any part of her and it would flop back like a rag doll.

"I've got to go in and see Tom. You must come with me."

She shook her head very slightly.

"I'm not leaving you here on your own."

If he had thought about it beforehand – which he hadn't – he realised now he would have expected hysterics, weeping. Not this.

"I'm sorry but there's something that needs Tom's decision – something that's got to be done quickly."

He went to the bedroom and got a jacket for her; she didn't object but stood up mechanically when he held it out and then put it on her.

"Got the key?"

"Does it matter," she said then.

They got a cab. In the cab she said, "So little time was given to us, Luke . . . April."

Luke couldn't bear to look at her.

Tom had gone back to the Institute; his face was grey like putty.

Mary stayed upstairs when Luke went down to the lab to see him.

"Would you rather stay up here?" he had asked her and taken her silence as assent.

"Tell me about it," said Tom.

After Luke had gone through it all once more, he asked why they hadn't told London straightaway over the intercom. "We thought you were unexpansive when it was all over . . . couldn't understand the silence from *you* . . . just getting Dotty."

Luke had realised that this was going to be difficult to answer.

He said, "I thought Mary ought to be told by someone on the spot – so that she knew everything had been done," he hoped it sounded understandable, but it didn't, not even to his ears, "and then there was this question of the man we've picked up. I obviously had to come home to talk to you. You realise what this means . . . we have to return him . . ."

Seeing Tom so crushed and defeated shook Luke to the core. He supposed he had always thought of Tom as a superman – made of granite – invincible. Had thought he could always lean on him. But now he couldn't. Tom was as vulnerable as anyone although up till now he had been able to disguise it. With a blow of this magnitude and just the two of them face to face, Luke was seeing the real Tom.

"Can we do it?" he said urgently.

Tom went over and leaned on the tachyon generator (Luke hated it with all his soul, hated it as much as he hated the submarine).

"I think we can, Luke. Even to finding the pole at the same exact point of time. I learned a lot yesterday. The trouble will be – and this seems ridiculous, but it's always the small things – getting the power from the Electricity Board."

"They'll not put anything in the way when they know there is a human being involved?" said Luke shocked.

"Can we afford to let them know what is involved? Just imagine the attraction if it leaked out. Someone from the fourth century B.C. We would never get him back unscathed."

Luke let his mind return briefly to the bundle of cloth in the torpedo room. Would the press ever be convinced that it was anything other than a hoax? He thought not. But it would be unthinkable to expose the man to anything like that.

"Simon is fairly well in with them – the Electricity people."

"Simon is going to be tricky."

"Did you ring him?"

Tom nodded.

"What was his reaction?"

"What is anyone's reaction to the loss of a close friend?"

"Sorry, I suppose what I mean is, did he blame us?"

"Yes," said Tom briefly. Then, "But he was restrained. We, after all, are to blame."

Luke said levelly, "That is perfectly true."

They talked of scientific details then because they both felt that if they didn't they might slide into some kind of chasm from which they would never climb out.

Luke said, "The *Artemis* is proceeding to Haifa tomorrow. That was part of her routine plan and the Captain saw no reason for being diverted from it. We are quite extraordinarily lucky with him; he is a marvellously sympathetic man and one hundred percent behind us. I agreed with him that it was pointless hanging about where we were. I am going to join the submarine again when they are in port the day after tomorrow. If you agree, we can produce the Humboldt Effect not too far from there and take the man into shore. We now know the extent of the area that is likely to be affected."

"How do you propose to get him ashore?"

"In the gemini dinghy."

"That will involve crossing the Time Barrier. We don't know this can be done."

"He's proved it can by coming out. The children in the first experiment three years ago crossed the Time Barrier unharmed."

"We have obviously got to take the risk," Tom said. "But it's highly dangerous."

"Does anyone doubt that anything connected with this business is dangerous?"

Tom said nothing for a moment. Luke, his voice choked with emotion, said, "Which makes it all the worse that Arthur had an ordinary accident which could have been prevented."

With great emphasis Tom said, "Don't." Then, after a pause he said bleakly, "I haven't even thanked you for what you have done. It all went through superbly."

"You know quite well I would rather have failed a thousand times on that score and have Arthur back with us."

"We said before we went into it that we accepted the dangers. It was not carelessness; just because the unspeakable's happened in an unexpected way, we still have to accept it." He went over to get a telephone directory and leafed through the pages. "If we are to keep to your plan we must get on straightaway with the repeat performance. You realise, of course, that there's an alternative open to us."

"It is unthinkable not to return this chap to his right time."

Tom nodded. "Okay. But someone has to take him in the dinghy."

"I will."

"Can we spare you, Luke?"

"Could we spare Arthur?" said Luke. "There is no question of anyone else going."

Tom sensed that to Luke this gesture was a kind of expiation. He wished he himself could do something so positive; but he knew he was vital in London.

"Right. You drop this fellow in Haifa. It must have been some kind of fishing port even in those times. He will be able to get back to where he came from." Like Luke he felt no curiosity about the man.

The next half hour was spent discussing technical details; there was even less room for any discrepancies this time.

He woke in the night dragged out of a deep exhausted sleep; and heard her weeping, a wild gasping kind of weeping that went on and on. In one way he was relieved; her utter silence – blankness – had frightened him to death. It seemed not her; and not being herself, he was afraid that she might harm herself. He remembered his mother saying that grief had a pattern – she was a great one for analysing things – was the weeping the next stage after the silence?

He didn't know whether to go to her. He half got out of bed.

But he thought perhaps grief of this dimension should be private; perhaps it *needed* to be. After all he could do nothing to help her. That was another thing that frightened him – that he could do nothing. He desperately wanted to go to her and then thought perhaps he wanted to go for the wrong reasons; his own comfort being among them. Did she blame him? When he had blamed himself for not calling Arthur back she had shaken her head vehemently, passionately, and said, "No, no."

All the same one never knew.

He sat on the edge of the bed in an agony of indecision.

Half an hour later still sitting there, and Mary still weeping, he knew he had to go to the lavatory; his bladder was bursting. He could have sworn he made no sound but even before he crossed the landing, the sobs suddenly stopped and Mary's voice said, uncertainly, "Luke?"

"Yes?"

"What are you doing?"

"Going to the lavatory."

When he came back, she was standing on the landing, shivering uncontrollably, clutching a towelling dressing gown round her, her eyes huge and dry as if the weeping had been tearless.

He said, hardly bearing to look at her because she seemed so much in need of comfort, "Why don't you have a bath. It might be soothing. And I'll make some tea."

He went into the kitchen which was surprisingly large for a flat and she, after some hesitation, must have taken his advice because he heard the bath water running.

He filled the kettle and lit the gas, watching how it leaped and then steadied, doing everything slowly and deliberately because he knew they must somehow get through this terrible night. He warmed the pot and held his hands round it. Then he searched the cupboard and found some teabags and put in three.

By the time Mary came in, the tea had stood long enough to infuse. She sat in the old armchair in the corner with her legs tucked up beneath her and Luke lodged himself on the glass table, a wedding present from Aunt Jennifer.

She said, "Thank you, Luke," and gave a long, shuddering sigh.

He twitched back the kitchen curtain and saw the moonlight had faded long since and that light was creeping over the Chiswick rooftops. There was a low rumble; the first tube train was starting, attic-high on its embankment at the end of the street. It was after four o'clock.

"Tube's starting." He only said it for something to say. It had no relevance. Would they spend their time over the next years just stating irrelevances?

Mary didn't answer and he doubted whether she had heard. The bath had taken away some of her pallor.

"Do you want another cup?" he said but saw then that she hadn't touched the first.

She said, "I knew it was going to happen."

"How could you?" – in surprise and disbelief.

"I should have said something. You blame youself for letting Arthur fall. I could have stopped him going."

"You couldn't have stopped him; how could you have stopped him? Not Arthur – he believed in it all utterly. What do you mean 'you knew' anyway?"

She didn't answer for a moment and then she said, in a low voice, "Those funny sort of . . . turns. D'you remember the first one in the Whale Hall and then the second one – that evening when Nick and Simon were here? I can remember it all now as clearly as if it had only just happened. Straight afterwards I couldn't, but since then it has come back to me, in the daytime, and in dreams at night."

"But you kept saying it was nothing."

"Arthur was so anxious about it all, especially the second time – and it seemed to me that he had other things on his mind, far more important. I didn't want to worry him further. It made it seem as if he had married a neurotic."

Of course Luke remembered that afternoon in the Natural History Museum; who would have forgotten? The second time it had been in the kitchen – here.

They had come to supper, he and Nick and Simon. Simon had been in one of his argumentative moods, stretched out on the sofa in the sitting room laying down the law. Luke had got up and gone into the kitchen to help Mary, sick to death of Simon's disagreements.

"Sorry," she had said, fairly hurling open cupboard doors and whisking furiously – like everything else she did, she cooked with *panache* – "Supper won't be a moment. Are they arguing?

Simon does nothing but argue these days but he usually improves with food."

He had improved considerably as they ate spaghetti covered with an exotic, creamy sauce.

When Nick had raised his glass and said, "Well, here's to a successful voyage," Simon had surprisingly raised his too.

"Bound to be good weather in the Med."

"Don't you believe it," Nick assured him. "I was on the Mediterranean coast for ten days last year and the red flag was flying every day. There was a real swell."

"A calm sea is ab-so-lutely essential for the experiment or the helium can't be laid . . ."

"In that case we'll have to sacrifice to the weather god. Make sure he's on our side!"

"Draw lots who's to be tipped overboard to appease the . . ."

"Draw your piece of spaghetti," bellowed Simon leaning across the table to where what was left of the first course sat in the cold casserole. "Shortest strand is the loser."

"NO!"

In surprise they had turned and looked at Mary. Only the moment before she had got up from the table to reach for something in the tall kitchen cupboard. She stood with her back to it. "Stop it," she cried. "Stop it. Stop it. Stop it." She was shouting like a fish wife.

Then she had frozen into inaction – looked at the four of them sitting at the table and yet not looked at them; didn't see them rather – for Luke remembered her face had emptied of anything that was happening in the kitchen. Mary had been seeing something elsewhere. As if she had thrown off her own identity, she stood like a member of the chorus, a watcher of some tragedy that she could not partake in but only suffer for.

Simon had said irritably, "Okay, okay, don't take on. We won't do it then. Only meant as a joke . . ." and he had leaned across the table and helped himself to another piece of french bread, buttering it slowly and deliberately and looking put out.

Arthur had got to his feet and gone quickly over and put his arm round her. "You all right, girl?"

But Arthur might not have existed for all Mary had looked through him to something beyond, something that was being enacted for her eyes only.

It had been uncanny, horrible; only lasting for a minute or two before she came to herself with a convulsive shudder, utterly bewildered . . . remembering, she had said at the time, nothing.

"What can you remember of it now?" Luke asked her quietly. "Or don't, if you would rather not."

"The first time it was the storm and the whale. And this man, who I thought was Arthur, tossed in the waves. Tossed like a piece of matchwood . . ." The tears started to run down her cheeks but she went on talking. "And then the second time it was a crowd of people drawing lots – like you were doing with the spaghetti – and as a result of it, they threw someone overboard. It was horrible" – she hid her face in her knees as if she saw it again in front of her – "it was a storm again, terrifying, enormous seas and rain. And I thought it was Arthur that time too, being flung out . . ."

"But Arthur wasn't flung out . . . not like that."

She was all hopelessly muddled in her mind. It must be some recurrent nightmare.

"What happened . . . what happened to this man you saw . . . this man you thought was Arthur?"

"I don't know. Oh, I don't know and that's the dreadful thing. If only I could see it through, then we might know. The awful thing, Luke, is not knowing. How can I go through the rest of my life not knowing what happened to him?"

"He couldn't have survived, Mary, in that sea. And I give you my word, we searched . . . for hours and hours. If he was alive, we would have found him. No one could swim in that."

She said, "One thing Arthur could do was swim. I found this out on our honeymoon. He's hopeless at any other kind of sport – totally uncoordinated. But his father was a channel swimmer – I don't expect he ever told you – and all the children were made to swim almost before they could walk."

"I had no idea; he never told me, no. Typical Arthur."

"If I tried to *see* something again, Luke. Do you think I could see what's happened to him?"

"Oh Mary!" All she would see, he was sure, would be Arthur on the sea bed. And to try and dabble in anything so suspect, so unscientific, went against all his principles.

"I can't think it's good to try and bring that kind of thing on ... "

"I'd do anything ... "

"Dear, dear Mary, I know you would."

She tried to *see* something in the early hours of the morning in the sitting room which faced west where the dark still lay in the corners under the eaves. The milkman was already rattling his bottles and carelessly playing his radio in the street below. She experienced nothing; until Luke pacing to and fro across the room, begged her to stop for it seemed to him that such 'turns' came only uncalled for. Hours later, although it was only two or three it seemed far more, she cooked him some breakfast for Luke had to get back to the airport. She was outwardly composed now although Luke, dead tired and silent eating his bacon and eggs, could only wonder for how long.

Then in a voice unbelievably tight, she said what Luke had been dreading. "If you picked up that man, Luke, from the Time Field, you realise what that means?"

"What?" He didn't look at her.

"Arthur ... too ... could have gone *in*."

"I promise you, Mary, I don't think he could. The man was swept out on these huge waves. It was running that way not the other ... "

"The sea can do extraordinary things ... "

"What can we do about that but believe it didn't happen," he said desperately.

She came over to the table and Luke sensed that her desperation dwarfed even his own.

"When you take that man back into his own time – take me. Take me so that I can look ... "

"What are you asking?" he shouted, "You'd just wander about – alone."

"Is there any difference where I wander alone – in this world or that world?" she cried.

"I hate leaving you," he said as they shut the outside door. She insisted on walking to the underground with him. "Promise me that you'll go to someone. Tom or home . . . "

"I'll not go home," she said. "They didn't understand Arthur. They didn't understand me for marrying him. And although they would be sympathetic, they'd be glad in their heart of hearts because they thought he wasn't my kind."

He stopped short and looked at her. "I know – Arthur's mother. Why not go to her. She'll need someone. Tom was ringing her last night."

"I might," said Mary slowly. "I'll see . . . I don't really know her. Arthur always said we would get on, once we knew each other . . . But I ought to do my job at the Institute if they are doing the experiment again."

"Nobody will expect you to do that."

"Luke," she said in the booking hall of the station, as though the thought had only just struck her. "Someone will have to take this man across the Time Barrier."

Luke pretended to adjust his canvas duffle bag. "Someone will," he said as casually as he could.

"*You* won't, will you, Luke . . ? I couldn't bear that . . . "

He could not find it in his heart to be truthful. "Don't worry, I don't know who will be going yet."

"You promise me . . . "

"I can't in all faith promise anything, Mary," he said and the words fell like pebbles in the quiet pool of the early morning, "except that I'll come back, don't worry . . . "

For the first time since he had arrived, she clung to him quite desperately. After a moment or two he disentangled himself gently and after kissing her, went off up the stairs to the platform, not looking back because he felt that if he did, it might be beyond his self control to leave her behind.

PART THREE

Chapter 8

August B.C.

Down, down ... pounded down; all the weight of the world pressing ... all the water of the universe choking ... struggle ... struggle ... fight to survive ... fight the pressure, fight the weight, fight the beating-the-life-out hammer blows of the huge wave.

Streaks of light flashed before Arthur's eyeballs. Drums beat in his ears. As a waterfall breaks a piece of matchwood, so the monstrous wall of water seemed bent on smashing him to the bottom of the sea.

But with an animal instinct to survive, he clawed his choking way upwards. Up ... up ... up to the top. If that way was up. Where was the top in this seething, throttling sea without breath ... life-taking, macerating, suffocating water ...

Gasp. Choke. Eyes full; ears full; whole body pain-wracked; as helpless as a piece of weed; a sponge sodden past saturation.

But flung up suddenly like a cork out of a bottle, he found himself choking this time on air, not water.

Relief was short-lived. Hardly had he spat once, drawn half a breath into his bursting lungs, before the next wave was battering. He tried to shout. "Hel ... ughle." Water poured into his open mouth. The pinnacles of foam hanging like a crown above him crashed downwards.

Keep your senses.

Dive, dive when it threatens to crush you. Thrash out despite the drumming. *Keep your senses intact*; fight back against the broiling turmoil.

Again a bursting chest, a cascade of lights searing his eyeballs.

Again he was under. Helpless. But still fighting – *just* fighting.

This time when he surfaced, he was lifted right up onto a crest. He shook his head violently, throwing back water and hair, narrowing painful eyes against an oncoming squall. That was all he needed. Rain.

But as he hung, totally exhausted for one motionless second, he saw the shape. The shape of a huge fish, wallowing. The submarine.

They were there – some distance away but there. They would pick him up as soon as they spotted him.

Make them see you.

Again he tried to shout but the salt had got his throat like gravel and no sound came. They would never hear anything anyway above the crashing of the sea.

The sea was calmer round the submarine. He must head in that direction, get clear of his immediate turbulence.

Arthur struck out with desperate urgency but even as he did so, another huge wave curled over from behind him, foam fingers clutching for his body. He was swept away again, backwards, away from the submarine, helplessly cursing . . .

And then he was swamped again.

Third time and you drowned. He should be dead now. Give up. Surrender to the sea. He could no longer struggle, had no more fight left in him. It was beyond human strength. *Give up*. There was, in fact, nothing in his mind as coherent as thoughts but merely instincts which guided his actions.

But still his exhausted brain insisted on ticking over. *Fight*. Make your limbs work . . . let them know you're here. They'll be looking . . . they were picking someone up . . . they'll pick you up too.

For in that brief moment he had seen figures on deck . . . one . . . two . . . three of them. And they were pulling something from the sea.

Then came the yellow light. It was like nothing that had gone before. It was no crashing of water but a cataclysm of sound apart.

Was it outside or inside his head? Arthur was past telling. The pressure was like nothing he had ever experienced before. How much longer could he survive the wracking pain in his chest; the drumming in his head; stabbing behind his eyes?

Was he still alive?

As the wall of sound and pressure fell away, Arthur became aware that he was; afloat on the surface and no longer fighting for air. The storm was abating and the water was slopping over his head not forcing him down. *He was breathing*, great rasping gasps.

If he was going to reach the submarine, now was his last chance.

He spat violently and the dry burning sensation left in his throat made him retch. He strained his eyes in the direction that he thought rescue lay.

But that last convulsion must have upset his bearings; the submarine was not where he thought he had previously seen it. He propelled himself painfully round.

Whichever way he looked, there was nothing.

God in heaven, had the sub gone?

Had it dived to get out of the storm?

Then Arthur knew real panic – the panic of being abandoned. Up till now, fighting the sea, fear had been a physical struggling thing. He had been occupied only with struggling. This was something far worse.

As he rode up and down on the swell automatically jerking up his head as a wave slapped his face, his movements to keep afloat became frantic and the whole empty sea ran together in a dizzy blur before his eyes.

He began to call out, "Luke, Luke!" but the sounds he made were moans of terror and the bitter, drying taste of salt in his mouth made him retch over and over again.

Then like a hand reaching down to him in a black pit, the thought came that Luke would never abandon him. Luke would not. He would be back. With the storm passing, the submarine would surface. It might be there now under his very feet in that measureless depth of green water between him and the bottom of the sea.

And meanwhile keep on top at all costs. *Preserve your strength.*

115

Lie on your back and float . . . rest . . . be there when they come.
He lost track of how long he floated there between sea and sky.
But as the day wore on, the black clouds scudded away towards
the horizon and the sky became white with heat. Yet the sea was
cold; ice cold if you had been in it for as long as Arthur. He lost the
feeling in his feet and hands; they became a third party, utterly
detached from him. Not only his limbs but his brain began to
grow numb though the skin on his face was soon tight with heat
from the fierce sunlight. Intense heat and fierce cold. The sea still
swelled and breathed with the after-effects of the storm and from
time to time, a wave washed over his face making him splutter
and choke.

A piece of flotsam saved him, flotsam that had come adrift from
some boat in the storm – an oar and a rough wooden box caught
together in a tangle of rope.

It bumped against his shoulder. He still had enough hold over
his mind to make himself roll towards it. He flung an unfeeling
arm over it; with a superhuman effort he thrashed his legs and
they obeyed him. He pushed his chest up out of the water,
gasping with pain. But he rolled onto the rope.

Hang onto that. Hang on until Luke comes. His limbs would
now no longer move; he couldn't make them find a more
tolerable position; they were heavy as lead. Heavy as dead . . .
lead.

He began to moan continuously. "Luke! Luke, boy. I can't hold
on for ever." And then more desperate: "Hurry for God's sake."

He closed his puffy eyelids against the sun but he could not
shut out the rays and the whole world was red and glaring . . . red
as blood. There would be no blood when he drowned, only his
bloated swollen body. In his confused state, he remembered a
hamster of his sister's that he had once drowned in a bucket of
water. He had been amazed how swiftly it had become puffed up
. . . unrecognisable as any kind of creature, a shapeless, swollen
pumpkin. In his imagination his body began to swell until he no
longer felt any separateness of parts but one fused swollen mass
that was flesh and spirit alike. He began to rail against Humboldt
whose only thought was his science. He must have given Luke

orders to leave the area. Luke on his own would not abandon him
. . . Tears of self pity and hopelessness rolled down his burning
face. The noise of his moans mingled with the little water noises
of waves slapping against his improvised raft. There were
seemingly no other sounds in this lonely sea.

He was picked up. He didn't know how much later. But it wasn't
by the submarine. Worse than his burning limbs, by this time was
his burning thirst.

He had no clear picture of the boat that picked him up, being
less than half-conscious. But after he had been flung down, none
too gently on deck and had lain inert for some time, he gradually
realised by the thrust of the water and the little grunts of exertion
somewhere above his head that he lay alongside men rowing.
Later he became aware of the creak and slap of a sail.

His eyes were gummed up with pain but he could listen and
there was plenty of noise after the silence of the raft. There were
men. People shouted and argued, the voices sharp and heated, in
a guttural tongue that had no familiarity. He must have indicated
that he wanted water to drink, for someone poured liquid down
his throat. Then he vomited, not once but over and over again, all
the sea water that he had swallowed forcing its way out. He was
hauled up roughly and his head pushed over the side. The hands
that held him dug into his flesh; they were calloused and horny –
sailors' hands, well used to hauling on ropes.

When at last his stomach stopped heaving, Arthur with a
supreme effort forced open his eyes. He looked at narrow
pointed features, a tangled beard. A very fierce kind of face.

But weak as Arthur was, it registered with him that though the
face was fierce, the man himself was afraid.

Why should he be afraid?

Even as Arthur looked at him, the man let go his supporting
hold and Arthur slid down, back into the body of the boat.

He was quickly surrounded by a whole group of men; dark
skinned, most of them bearded, wearing a kind of tunic or waist
cloth of rough linen. This puzzled Arthur although in his be-
fuddled state he could not think why it should. And the feeling

117

persisted that they, like the first man, were afraid of him. Only one stood a little apart; he had no beard. Arthur could feel him, still and watchful. When one of the other men put out a hand to finger his watch, the man pulled his sharply back.

The sailor was going to pinch it, was he – damn him; Arthur had had the watch from his mother for his twenty-first birthday and didn't feel charitable towards a thief. He let out a hiss and it bubbled between his swollen lips, but the man did not come near again. He said thickly, "Arthur Smith," trying to point to himself – a ludicrous and useless piece of information and quite lost on them for the sound of his voice only renewed their jabbering speculation and he wished he had kept quiet.

He indicated that he wanted another drink for his throat was unbearably dry and acid-tasting – but they didn't seem willing to co-operate. They continued to stare and argue; one man actually struck another in his agitation and Arthur didn't give much for his chances if they set on him.

But he was too physically demolished to worry about this and he wished they would leave him alone and settle their differences elsewhere; so he groaned and lay back and they pushed him quickly onto some bulging sacks then and left him. The sacks had a strange sweet smell; there were a great many of them on deck; but they weren't uncomfortable to lie on. The boat must be some kind of trader.

After a while, his breathing became easier but as feeling began to seep back into his limbs, every bone in his body gave him pain. Eventually he struggled to sit up, hoping to ease himself. This made the men gather round again. This time the beardless man thrust his face at Arthur – all teeth. He clicked his tongue and it seemed to Arthur there was menace in the small sound: it didn't sound friendly.

Someone pointed ahead and shouted a name. Arthur took it to mean that land lay in front; he himself could see nothing. They were making reasonably good way for although the wind was light, it filled the sail and this was augmented by a bank of half a dozen oars on each side of the ship. The man pointed and shouted again; there were answering shouts up and down the ship. Whatever land it was, they were making directly for it. As they came nearer in, the pitch of the men's voices sharpened, whether with excitement or apprehension there was no way of telling.

Then suddenly, when even Arthur could see a smudge of shore no more than a hundred yards off, the beardless one seized him. Four other men came to help. Arthur was thrust roughly towards the side of the boat.

Too late he realised their intentions. He tried to grab hold of a sack, a man's tunic – anything he could catch hold of. But in his weak state he was powerless. He would have been no kind of match for them anyway, outnumbered as he was.

They were going to push him back into the sea.

No. No. Not that. Anything but that.

Arthur screamed, desperately, despairingly.

Four pairs of hands held him by the arms and legs; slid him over the side; it was some way to fall. He went under like a stone when he hit the sea. And when he surfaced again, the boat had turned and, with a slapping sail, was being rowed rapidly up the coast. No one looked back.

He never knew how he reached the shore. Afterwards he marvelled at the stubborn instinct of self-preservation which prevails over utter agony and exhaustion; and refuses to give in to the voice which promises peace . . . if you let the water take you . . .

That he survived was due largely to the sea here being calm and warm; a trace of its previous violence and he would have been finished instantly.

As it was, his heart bursting through his ribs, he lived to feel land – solid land scraping his knees under the sea as a beach shelved down to meet him. The sea lifted him gently onto the sand, dry gritty sand that stuck to his cheeks and lips as he lay with his head just above the water line and could make no effort to go further. The sea lapped at him, up and down, gently filling his tee shirt like a balloon and then falling away so that it clung to his back in tight wet wrinkles. Just another bit of flotsam from the storm.

It was only when a swell more vigorous than usual came up and slopped into his mouth, making him choke and setting off another bout of painful wracking sickness that he roused himself to crawl, his head hanging like a dog, into the shadow of some stunted bushes.

He succumbed then to total exhaustion and slept for several hours, a disturbed moaning sleep from which he was woken by the sound of Mary calling.

"Arthur!"

"It's no good," he said, "I'm done for."

But she didn't seem to understand. "Arthur . . . come on."

He saw her in a cloud of golden sunlight which burnished the reddy flecks in her hair; she was wearing the flower-sprigged blouse that he liked . . .

"Come and help me then," he said.

But she laughed improbably and bent down, fumbling with something in front of her. Then she began to walk away, totally unconcerned.

"Wait!" he shouted in helpless frustration. "Wait!" But when he listened to the sound he made, it was unrecognisable as a word. She wouldn't realise he was calling. He jerked himself upright to run after her.

The beach stretched empty in front of him. The intense heat had gone out of the day and the sun was sliding down the sky towards the horizon.

Water. He must find water to quench his raging thirst. His tongue was swollen and clumsy and altogether too big for his mouth. He sank back with a sigh into a sea of aches and pains.

Think man. Rouse yourself. Where are you?

Mary, unreal as she had turned out to be, had nevertheless done the trick – woken him up – made him face his predicament. What he'd give for a long drink of water and three or four aspirins. His mind began to move back slowly and with difficulty over what had happened.

The experiment. The Humboldt Effect. It had worked. He was sure of that; hadn't he seen time slipping backwards on the chronometer? There had been a storm; a man flung out of a ship. And then he had gone too – into that turbulent sea.

Here his memory clammed up – or shied away. It was all too recent – too unthinkable. They hadn't picked him up; the submarine had gone off . . .

But another boat had. The memory of sailors in a kind of Biblical tunic bothered him. They had pushed him out into the sea again, albeit well in sight of land. And he'd struggled to this beach.

Men were swine.

What beach for God's sake?

He held his aching head. He must, if he took time and thought slowly, be able to work out what beach. During those days on board the *Artemis* when they had had so little to do, they had looked at the map a great deal. Talked about Israel which lay thirty odd miles or so to the east of them because it was Dotty's country. She knew a great deal about Israel; had spent a year on a *kibbutz* before coming to the Institute and had holidays there in the years since.

He knew the exact position of the *Artemis* due west of Tel Aviv when the Humboldt Effect took place; he could plot the grid reading as accurately as he could their flat in Chiswick. He wouldn't have moved too far from that spot when he was picked up, not more than a mile or so at the most. And the lugger type boat had made for the coast with the wind directly behind it.

Which made the beach where?

What had they said when they pointed at land. Something like Yoppa. *Jaffa!* Jaffa was the docks area of Tel Aviv – or some part of it anyway. If they *had* sailed due east (here he tried to wet his finger with his parched tongue and hold it up to the wind; yes, it was coming straight off the sea as near as he could tell), then he must be in the vicinity of Tel Aviv now. And Tel Aviv was enormous; its suburbs stretched for miles north and south along the coast. Surely he wouldn't have to go too far before he could find help of some kind. As it got darker he would see the glow of its lights in the sky which would tell him the direction he must take.

He could find a hotel, he thought hopefully, despite the fact that he hadn't a penny in his pocket, nor, of course, a passport. Things would have to be arranged. He would have to get to a British Consulate and tell them who he was; at least they could check up on him pretty quickly; contact the *Artemis*. If he got on a plane going back to London, instead of going back to the submarine, he might even be home before the rest of them. A wave of homesickness swept over him. That waking dream of Mary had brought him back to consciousness but it had made him realise how much he needed her sympathy. A jab of pain behind his eyes made him groan.

He rubbed them; they pricked abominably and stung with salt. They were as sore as hell.

But the irritation in the right eye was more pronounced than the left; it felt like a grain of sand under the lid. Clumsily he lifted his lid away from his eyeball. All at once his sight improved. As if he had a lens in his eye, a smeary salty lens.

Then he realised what had happened and he gave a croak of a laugh. *His contact lens*. One of them was still there. Instead of coming out in the sea, it had gone up under his eyelid as they sometimes did and stuck there and now, rubbing his eye, he had pushed it back into place.

What luck! At least he could see in a lop-sided way. He closed his eyes, one at a time, experimentally. Yes. Although the beach was a pretty good blur out of his left eye – out of his right, he could see it in clear detail now. He blessed Mary for making him change from glasses to lenses. Glasses in that sea would have lasted two seconds.

What a commercial he could write for the opticians when he got back. *Sticks to your eye-ball even through a cataclysm in time*. More than could be said for his watch which in its acutely waterlogged state had lost one of its hands.

A lonely cry of a bird was borne down the wind. Now he could see so much better he could size up his position.

After the bird's cry there wasn't another sound. It was quiet as death. The beach stretched away in a long straight line in both directions as far as the eye could see in the green evening light.

Behind the beach were the dunes. The sea hardly moved, save for a little frill of foam at the edge that turned itself over with scarcely a whisper. A golden sunset had not materialised, the sun having dropped into thin cloud on the horizon. The only real noise in the world was the rasp of his painful breathing and the dry slurp of his tongue when he swallowed. Even the wind had died. If he hadn't the evidence of his battered body, he would have found it hard to believe the monstrous storm of a few hours before.

Dotty was wrong about the beaches; he would have to tell her. She had said they were ruined in Israel; covered in barbed wire and patrolled by soldiers because of the ever-present threat of invasion. There were no empty, peaceful beaches left, according to Dotty. Nowhere could you forget that Israel was a country besieged, surrounded by neighbours ready to pounce.

And yet here was sand that might have been virgin; never trodden by man. Not a single scrap of newspaper blew among the stunted bushes; there was no sign of a plastic sandwich wrapper, or old beach chair; not a suggestion or a hint. Coast so near to civilisation and yet completely unspoilt? The lights from Tel Aviv would be showing soon, if his calculations were right. He thought they must be – roughly anyway.

But Dotty. Dotty was worrying.

Dotty was a very accurate person.

In such a densely populated country would any beach be so completely unexploited – so completely deserted on a warm evening in August in the 1980s?

He scanned the sky. You would expect to see planes about in a defence-conscious country. Now he thought about it, he couldn't remember seeing a plane since he had gone overboard from the *Artemis*.

He didn't want to follow the road his mind was taking. He wanted to branch off, double back, escape in any other direction . . . he dug in his toes.

But a little nucleus of fear swelled, refused any longer to be ignored and all in a second detonated and exploded, lighting up the darkest recesses of his subconscious. It uncovered fear that he did not know he possessed and terrified him far more completely and destructively than the sea had ever threatened to do.

Whose time was he in?

His own time . . .

Or the time of the experiment?

He began to shake uncontrollably. His teeth chattered and waves of nausea shook him to the marrow. For a moment he gave way to sheer animal panic. With a strength he could not have mustered five minutes before, he ran stumbling and panting up the beach back up to the sand dunes and scrabbled like a maniac towards the top, slipping and sliding in the sand and making hardly any headway at all. He merely exhausted himself. The pain in his chest became crippling and he collapsed before he reached anywhere near the top, moaning and tearing at the sand with his hands.

He made it in the end but by now the light was fading in earnest and at the top of the dune, he could only see the rounded outlines of other dunes folding into the distance behind and on both sides, giving no clue as to where he might be. He felt then that he hadn't the courage to survive. That it would have been preferable a thousand times over to have drowned out there in the sea than to be faced with his present predicament.

But the mind cannot exist for too long on this high pinnacle of terror; it must either go over the top or become controllable and after a while, although the fear was undiminished, he stopped his limbs shaking by knotting his muscles tautly against himself. He tasted blood on his lips and found that he had been biting them savagely in his fraught state of mind, cracked and dried as they were by the salt.

His thirst was unbearable. He must find water.

Even in these unthinkable circumstances, Arthur found he had an instinct to survive. Now his whole mind became obsessed with the need for water.

There would be no water in the dunes; he must get behind them. He set out away from the sea. His progress was miserably slow. To conserve what little strength he had he did not climb the dunes but went round the bottom where he could, and in-between. Even so there were times when he had to climb and then he thought that his end had come. But each time he fell he somehow managed to get up again and his body crawled on.

Darkness fell – but after an hour the moon came up and there was light enough to follow some kind of course. He mumbled *water, water* as he went as if by forming the sound, it might help to make it a reality.

He was beginning to think he was wandering in a circle, aimlessly, had fallen five times in as many minutes and was at last losing the will to crawl on again, when he came out between two dunes and he was through them.

The land rolled away, going slightly downhill and there were bushes, though dry and stunted, and a sand-encrusted tree. There was a different smell in the air; just a suggestion of greener things where before he had smelt only hot dry sand – a suggestion so faint that it might be his muddled imagination.

But under the roots of a second tree, he found the smallest thread of water dripping into an indentation among the pebbles in a gully of rocks. The bed of a stream all but dried up in the height of summer. He shaped his hands into a cup but his thirst far outstripping the slow dripping of the water, he found in the end it was more effective to drop his head and drink like an animal. He gulped slowly and laboriously for a long time.

After that he had had his lot. He crawled under some bushes and slept. And as the bushes on the beach had protected him from the worst of the sun in the afternoon, so these acted as some kind of protection against the chill of the night.

He woke only a few hours later, unwilling and shivering. Having slept in his contact lens, his eye was puffy and even more painful; but his stiff and aching limbs had more strength and he felt generally more *compos mentis*.

But that was hardly an advantage under the circumstances; better to be unconscious than to be able to dwell rationally on the situation.

Christ! What a mess he was in.

Even as he said this without any intention to blaspheme, a thought came to him as a final crushing blow. If the chronometer on the submarine was to be believed, he was in a world that knew nothing of Christ.

Uncommitted to any specific creed, Arthur nevertheless felt this spelled out the very essence of bleakness and isolation. It produced a numbness in his mind which might well have been the beginning of the end.

As it was some small sand creature nipped the flesh of his calf and in an automatic gesture of brushing it off, he heard someone say. *You're as good as done for if you don't get up.*

The illusion was so complete that he scrambled to his feet and looked round for the owner of the voice.

It could only have been his own. But once on his feet, he noticed the dawn light green and yellow in the sky to the east; his clothes were sopping wet with dew and he needed to find something to eat. He began to follow the runnel of the dried up stream to see if it led him to more bushes where there might be wild fruit.

No wonder the men who had picked him up in the trader had been alarmed; he must have seemed to their unsophisticated eyes an extraordinary figure in his torn jeans and ragged Batman tee-shirt; what on earth would they have made of that winged figure on his chest? He reckoned he was lucky to have escaped with his life.

He came upon a single tree growing out of a cranny by a pile of stones. On its branches were half a dozen wizened fruits which he could only think were figs. At home he would never touch a fig. He ate every one of these that he could find. The very fact of eating was a kind of tranquillizer. He sat on a stone to think.

To survive even for a short time he had to have a plan. Something to follow. He knew now that more dangerous by far than hunger and thirst, was fear – losing his reason through fear of isolation, fear of abandonment. He had to go over every possible escape route and pretend there was one even if it didn't exist.

He was a scientist. His winning card – his *only* card – was his ability to work things out. If he let his emotions get on top so that he was no longer capable of clear thought, he had had his lot. *I'm not beaten yet.*

To contact the submarine. That was the only hope of returning to the twentieth century. Would Luke come back and search? It was scientifically possible to plot the same location; carry out the same time reversal. How would he know that Arthur had survived? What use to Arthur that Luke returned at an unspecified time, thirty miles out in the Mediterranean at some place west of Tel Aviv when here he was behind the coast with no means of putting to sea.

That line of thought led nowhere.

The fruit he had eaten rolled in his stomach so that he doubled up with pain; the eye with the lens was so sore that he took the lens out and bathed his whole face in the trickle of water. It was while he was doing this that he thought he heard a shout. But after a moment of listening when he caught nothing but the dry sound of wind in the grass, he put it down to imagination.

It came again. As the solitude of the land had frightened him before, now he was afraid of any kind of human contact. The sound in the early morning had probably carried far. Nevertheless he looked round to see where he could hide. He saw an outcrop of grey stones and lay down behind them. The shouts came nearer.

A camel train. The camels came over the horizon, roped together, nose to tail, loaded with sacks and bundles and tent poles lashed on top. If Arthur had been nursing any hopes that he had made a mistake about the century he was in, those hopes were shattered. In front was a man on an ass, his loose garments flapping against the animal as he rode. There were others on foot, walking beside the camels and it was their cries he had heard first. Every so often they would whack one of the beasts and it would toss its head with its curling lip and take a few quick steps after the camel in front before rolling back, throwing out its feet in its normal slow shambling gait.

They must travel in the early hours to avoid the heat. Were they traders going south to Egypt? Arthur had a vague idea from days of junior school history that Israel around this time lay between the great trading powers of Assyria and Mesopotamia in the north, and Egypt and Arabia in the south.

The train was long; it took some time to pass and did not come too close. Close enough however for him to hear a camel cough and get rapped by its owner. They seemed to reserve a particular harsh tone for their beasts of burden.

After they had gone, Arthur put up a hand to his face and found he was sweating.

Was it all the result of a feverish imagination; had he peopled this Hebrew backcloth with a cast of extras as if from some great Biblical epic? But there was none of the sterilised glamour of the movies about those queer old robes or their dirty ill-tempered owners. And when a five minute walk brought him to the actual camel track, the dung on the path was real enough and the acid reek of animals hung heavily in the air.

His worst fears were confirmed that he was in an alien time.

Yet something nagged at the back of his mind as if he was failing to make some connection.

All of a sudden he made it. Those men with the flowing robes. They reminded him of the man tossed into the sea by his companions from the sailing boat at the time of the Humboldt Effect. *The man that was picked up by the submarine when they had failed to pick up him.*

LUKE HAD ON BOARD THE *ARTEMIS* A MAN FROM FOURTH-CENTURY ISRAEL.

The thought printed itself on Arthur's mind in capitals.

If this was so, they *must* be returning – and returning to the coast. They would hardly drop the man off in the middle of the sea.

And as if his brain had now firmly clicked into this track of thought, it ran on unimpeded. From the lowest level of despair, he rose to the heights of delirious hope.

Again he saw the man deliberately thrust overboard into the storm; the submarine wallowing like a whale and the man being pulled on board . . .

The man was Jonah.

Jonah swallowed up in the storm by the great fish.

In the end it was neither reasoning, nor science; it was pure intuition. It burst upon him like a great light at the end of a tunnel.

They had carried out the Humboldt Effect in an area of sea some way from Tel Aviv which centuries before had been the ancient sea port of Joppa – and time had rolled back and the poles had locked at probably the one and only bit of drama that had ever taken place there. Jonah, fleeing from Joppa, thrown overboard by the sailors, had been picked up by the twentieth-century submarine, which must have appeared to his frightened and untechnological eye as nothing but a great fish.

Was it too fantastic or simple enough to be the right explanation?

Arthur knew he was right.

His mother had been a staunch churchgoer; from the time he was five until he was ten, Arthur had sat on a hard straight-backed chair in the Sunday school hall behind the ugly stone church in the northern town where they lived; week after week a little lady in a soft felt hat had got them drawing pictures – Arthur remembered quite clearly the whale on the blackboard in the church hall. They had all had to copy it.

But the lady had gone further; she had drawn Jonah sitting outside the walls of a city – there had been some plant whose leaves were difficult to draw.

Jonah, after his trials in the belly of the whale, had repented that he had been trying to run away from God and had gone back to the wicked city of Nineveh.

"And it vomited out Jonah upon the dry land."

The Sunday school lady hadn't quite liked the word 'vomited' although it was a Bible word, she had said it quickly.

After three days in the belly of the fish, Jonah had returned to Israel. Knowing exactly what was involved, Arthur worked out that three days was just about the time they would need to re-equip the lab in London and the *Artemis* for a repeat of the experiment.

Where, oh where would Luke put the man down?

There must be a sensible answer.

Arthur beat himself into a frenzy of thought. He knew the

naval programme for the *Artemis* involved going on to Haifa. Would they set up the experiment there? It seemed a reasonable assumption. Arthur's photographic memory served him well. He knew from looking at the map with Dotty in the wardroom that at Haifa the straight coastline curved round a point into a bay where the mountains came close to the sea.

It was logical; as deductive as Arthur could be under the circumstances, always supposing that his intuition was correct. And as he had no other hypothesis to go on, he might as well assume that it was. It gave him hope if nothing else – something to go for.

But having worked things out this far was only half of it – the easier half. Where was *he* placed in Israel? And could he possibly get as far north as Haifa in the rather less than three days now left to him.

Once again he pictured Dotty's map and put himself somewhere in the region of Tel Aviv–Joppa. He might have sixty miles to go, perhaps more if he was unlucky; in little more than forty-eight hours.

It sounded a savage proposition. He had no shoes. He was weak and unfit and hungry; unlikely to find anything but fruit to eat. The heat of the day would be such that he would have to rest up and travel by night. He would have to avoid contact with any other travellers who might take a dislike to him. At least this clear-marked camel track seemed to be going north and would give him something to follow.

And the hills – which he could see here as a low shadow far over in the east where the rapidly lightening sky gave substance to their outline – would gradually curve round to the coast as he got further north; until where the mountain ran almost into the sea with only a narrow piece of land between, would be Mount Carmel and Haifa where he must hope to meet Luke. At that point you should see a good sweep of coastline . . . be able to attract attention.

He had no time to waste.

He had been beside himself with fear – he was appalled to think of it – so now he was beside himself to get started on his way. His heart was thumping against his ribs like a traction engine because he had a slender ray of hope where it had seemed there was absolutely none. His body responded; hardly able to drag himself along before, he could now walk upright. He was no longer crippled by the pains in his chest and legs. They would no doubt come back anon but for the moment mind dominated over matter. Make the most of it. He began to tear off the bottom of his ragged jeans and bind his feet; ineffectual in the long term, but it might cushion his soles until they hardened up a bit. Was he likely to encounter wild animals or snakes on this arid coastal strip behind the dunes? He twisted a thick bit of branch off a nearby tree.

Only then did he allow himself to think of Mary. Made stupid as he had been by the sea, cold, broken and despairing – to think about Mary when he had no hope of getting back to her was past enduring. He had closed a door in his mind; shut her out.

But now he needed her image to keep him going. As the dishevelled figure set off on his solitary way north, he was not alone. Solidly there in his mind's eye, Mary walked on the track in front of him.

"I'm following up behind this time," he said aloud.

PART FOUR

Chapter 9

September

"What are we hanging about for then?"

"Give us a chance; we can't go in before ITR."

"The sooner the better, I'd say ..."

"It won't be long now," Luke said calmly. He was quite amazed at his own calm.

There were three of them in the gemini dinghy, himself, Barry Lambert and the man from the fourth century. They had had to propel the Israelite forcibly out of the torpedo room and up on to the casing. He had made no effort himself. He must be pretty weak from lack of food, Luke reckoned.

When he had told the team of his intention to go back through the Time Field, Barry had said, "I'll come too."

Luke looking at him with dislike had instantly wondered at his motive. Relations between them had been frigid since Luke's return. It crossed his mind fleetingly that Barry wanted to do him in. But that, he had no doubt, was getting over-dramatic. There was a cat-like wariness about Barry, he had all his claws out; but maybe it was the one way he could offer the olive branch. It was the nearest that he could get to an apology.

Most likely his offer was sheer bravado. It fitted.

"There's really no need to come," Luke said stiffly. "No one knows the effect of crossing the Time Barrier. Just because this one man has done it, doesn't mean we can all get away with it."

"You might need help," Barry said stubbornly. "What if the chap gets awkward – or the outboard conks out?"

The morale of the Institute was at a low ebb; they all dreaded the repetition of the experiment, Luke more than any. Now,

135

unexpectedly, Nick backed up Barry; he thought it better that two of the team should go in the dinghy.

Luke shrugged and consented. He had no desire to make an issue out of it at this stage. The whole thing was proving pretty tricky; it was touch and go whether the authorities would allow the scientists to carry out the experiment again so near the coast. The Captain was invaluable; diplomatic when negotiating, and with friends in high places. There was endless communication with London. The electricity people were sticky about them using such a colossal load in the middle of the week.

They hadn't been entirely above board as to why they wanted to repeat the Humboldt Effect so soon. "Rush it through before anyone has time to ask questions," was William Bradley's advice. Excellent advice under the circumstances.

They made no contact with the Israeli fellow in the three days they had him on board; he remained in a kind of trance, on his knees for most of the time but periodically collapsing from total exhaustion. He neither acknowledged their presence nor responded when they tried to communicate. Luke thought it better and more humane to leave him alone; they had done enough harm to him already. The longer they kept him, the greater the danger of people finding out about him; the bigger the temptation to use him as some kind of scientific guinea pig. Both the Captain and Luke were adamant that as few people as possible should know of his existence.

The outboard motor popped as they throttled it back.

With two of the team in the dinghy – and without Arthur – they had had to re-assign jobs on board the *Artemis*. Nick was at the console on the casing. How safe it looked there, thought Luke. How could he ever have felt alone and exposed in such a position; why, it was an absolute plum compared to where he was now.

Not a plum for Arthur.

Luke shoved his mind hard on to another tack. The precipice yawned; he was within a hairsbreadth of disaster if his thoughts went that way. Barry, seeing Luke's face bare with emotion, wondered what awful image he was tussling with; but then his

Chapter 9: September

looks were under control and he was saying sharply, "Sit further
forward, Barry."

Graham and Sheila passed them going back from the helium
tent; waved silently. They could feel the team's tremendous
support.

"What'll it be like in there?"

"I wish I knew," said Luke. Barry had guts, one had to admit
that. He was keeping his panic well out of sight though it had to
be there. Very cool he was playing it.

"I'll let her idle," Luke said and cut the engine back more. "I
think when we're through the Time Barrier, the *Artemis* will
appear to be inside the canopy. A kind of reversal situation."

"*When* we're through . . . "

What came first? Pain . . . sickness . . . disorientation?

"Beginning to regret your noble offer?" Luke knew it was
mean, but he thought meanness at that moment might do more
than sympathy to steel Barry's nerve.

"No," Barry said and scowled. "I just hope the radiation
doesn't kill us."

"Don't we all. Right. Look out, I'm going in." They were very
near the canopy now.

Over the stornophone they could hear the final checks and call
of the countdown.

"One minute to go."

The longest minute in Luke's life. But paradoxically his fear left
him. He looked at the man huddled in the bows of the dinghy and
the bitterness he had felt towards him for taking Arthur's place
evaporated. He even felt a pang of regret that he had made no
effort to know the man; at another time – in another age – they
might even have had something in common; he might have liked
him a great deal more than he liked Barry Lambert. He saw that
under the damage wrought by the sea and three days' fasting, the
man's face had a quiet resignation; an acceptance of fate. He
might not be as old as he had at first appeared . . .

5, 4, 3, 2, 1, zero . . .

The agonising moment of limbo.

Then the first light.

137

"Taking her through," he shouted and Barry clutched the side of the dinghy as they leaped forward into what might be oblivion. "Shut your eyes," his voice rose to a scream as the world erupted and they fell into an endless void. He didn't know then if his courage would hold out.

'How long' he decided didn't mean a thing. The dinghy had been hurled – had fallen – had been struck some kind of tremendous blow?

He wasn't at all sure afterwards, being too intent at the time on keeping hold of the tiller under all circumstances. Perhaps the tides weren't the same; the sea level different.

Then they were through. The waves were choppy but perfectly manageable and the sun was warm on his face. Barry was grinning like an idiot and pointing towards the shore. Where there had been the distant port and buildings on the cliffs, they were now looking at a completely isolated coastline. Only the shape of Mount Carmel against the early morning sky was the same. Despite the sun, the skin on the back of his neck went cold and Luke felt the hairs on his legs prickle.

"Open her up! Go for it like hell!"

They had perhaps ten minutes, fifteen at the most, before the power failed and the time bridge collapsed, leaving them stranded.

The engine rose in a scream to full power and the dinghy reared to breast the sea, a white bow wave flung high in a cloud of spray.

The Israelite, who had collapsed somewhere under a thwart, scrambled to his feet. He clung onto the side of the dinghy for dear life, his eyes fixed rigidly on shore as if, after all he had been through, they were not to be trusted in what they saw.

As Luke throttled down and they slid into the beach, his eagerness to get out of the boat was matched only by Luke's eagerness to be rid of him. He was over the side with the boat still moving, and nearly flat on his face in the sea. He recovered himself and was wading forwards, stumbling and splashing without a backward glance.

"Thank auntie for the ride then," Barry shouted after him.

"Look out, I'm turning!" Luke was curt, cursing Barry and his wit. A hundred and eighty degrees sharp. "Shove her off with that pole . . . "

Barry pushed, taking his time, unabashed by Luke's obvious irritation. "Ugh – the original wet. Shovelling pebbles with his fingers . . . "

"Just might . . . be glad . . . to be back," Luke grated. He was watching the sharp curve of the dinghy, concentrating on the turn, not looking at the shore.

He'd be glad to be back too. So nearly home and dry, in the most real sense, and yet still the worst part to come; the tension if anything mounting. They must have at least seven minutes left.

The turn was too sharp, it threw Barry sideways and they shipped a lot of water. Barry, balanced once more, went back to watching the Israelite. He had binoculars round his neck and braced himself against the thwart of the leaping dinghy.

"Been spotted by a mate already," he shouted. "There's someone coming down like the clappers, straight down the rocks; God, he's a maniac! He'll break his ruddy neck. Let's hope Old Wailey shows him a bit more enthusiasm than he did us."

"No!" the glasses held unsteadily, "Wrong! Number Two's not taking a blind bit of notice of our wet friend . . . he's yelling . . . seems more interested in us . . ."

"For Pete's sake, Barry . . . " Luke, screwing up his eyes against the wall of spray, was trying to calculate the distance to the canopy and the *Artemis*. The submarine looked small and faint. "Look where we're going, can't you, you fool . . . not back . . . "

"Luke!"

"Christ! Can't you . . . ?"

"Look! Look! Take the glasses. Slow down. The chap there . . . shouting . . . "

"We don't want any more of them," shouted Luke in his turn, really angry now, "What did we come here for . . . to pick up some more . . . ?"

"I'll take the tiller," said Barry violently and pushed Luke off it, thrusting the glasses at him and nearly knocking him over. "It just looks like bloody Arthur!"

Barry had already throttled back when a white-faced Luke said in an incredulous, shaking voice, "Put her round. Back to the beach . . . flat out."

The dinghy swung round for a second time and more water poured in as they banked far too steeply. Luke hurled himself over to distribute the weight and by a miracle they avoided overturning.

"Be ready to go astern if it's not him . . ." He tried to keep the striding, shouting figure in the lens. "But it is, it is," he said under his breath . . .

The figure reached the edge of the beach while the dinghy was still some way out and threw himself into the sea, swimming like a crazy dog and not ceasing to shout. By the time they reached him he was spent.

"All right. We've got you!"

Arthur clutched hold of the side of the dinghy, gasping and retching. The whole boat tipped. Luke, with little regard for any of their safety, clutched at him wildly. He grasped his hands, his arms, got hold of him under the armpits. Barry, throwing himself the other way, yelled, "You'll have us in the drink between the two of you."

The sodden mass that was Arthur had no strength to help himself. He tried to kick his legs and they refused to function. Slowly, inch by painful inch, Luke dragged him up until his waist was over the transom. Then he grasped his legs and Arthur rolled into the bottom of the boat. Even safely there, Arthur clutched Luke as if he might disappear. Barry opened the throttle and they were back on course, heading towards the canopy and the *Artemis*.

Luke was appalled by the sight of Arthur. His face was hollow and his eyes cavernous and bloodshot. He had always been thin but now he looked a spectre of himself. Only a vestige of shirt clung to his back and his jeans were in shreds. Blood from cuts on his feet ran in little watery rivulets down the boards of the dinghy.

"Take your time," said Luke and tears rolled down his face. "No need to talk."

But Arthur had to. He couldn't wait, "I knew you'd come, Luke. I knew you'd be . . . back for me." He coughed up a lot of sea water and couldn't speak; then he shook his head violently and wheezed. "Mary . . . ?"

"She'll be glad to see you . . . God, Arthur . . . "

"Landed . . . Jonah then," Arthur twisted round with difficulty and pointed back to the shore as if seeing the man there for the first time; as if he hadn't noticed him before in his maniacal rush to attract Luke and Barry.

"Jonah?"

"Prophet . . . Jonah . . . picked him up in the sub . . . the whale . . . "

"What on earth?"

"S'why I'm here . . . worked it out . . . you'd be back in three days . . . to land Jonah . . . or I'd be sitting on my arse . . . in Israel for the rest . . . of my life . . . "

Arthur's eyes were bright with fever. Best thing was to humour him and get him to the Doc. He followed Arthur's gaze and saw the Israelite they had landed had now left the beach and was hurrying towards the deserted headland. Jonah?

"It looked like a fish . . . wallowing in that sea . . . he'll be telling people . . . and the story'll come down. . . " the words poured out of Arthur, thick and stumbling.

"Okay, Arthur. Take it easy. Wait and tell Mary."

"Mary," he said. "Kept me going. All the way. I'd not have made it without her."

"Of course you wouldn't. Relax. We've got to get through the Time Field. Let's cope with that."

But it wasn't possible for Arthur to stop. After three days of thinking he would never talk to anyone again, his relief made him into a robot that wouldn't switch off.

"Three days I had . . . I knew . . . I guessed at Haifa because of the submarine. I walked north . . . and hoped . . . the walk was bad . . . I kept going all night, some of the day too . . . the day was bad for walking . . . I found an old piece of cloth near a village . . .

it was foul . . . stinking . . . but it covered me so I looked like one of *them* . . . . then I had some luck" (he was shivering violently now) "another camel train . . . it had trouble with a camel and while they were sorting it out . . . I tied up one of their asses . . . in a thicket and they went away . . . without it . . . "

"Oh Arthur!" Hopelessly vague, impractical Arthur who couldn't act like that to save his life had proved that he could.

"So then I had an ass to ride . . . darn uncomfortable . . . and stubborn . . . was it stubborn! . . . I lashed it with a stick, Luke . . . I was frantic and I kept falling asleep . . . but it covered the ground where my feet wouldn't . . . couldn't . . . I saw you . . . in the dinghy . . . . I was too far over the hill . . . I thought you weren't going to see me . . . " He shivered more violently, went on shivering, ". . . all that way . . . and effort . . . and to miss you . . . "

His voice was giving out at last, croaking to a halt. It was impossible to hear him above the noise of the outboard.

"Barry saw you. If it hadn't been for him . . . "

At that moment Barry shouted. Luke, taken up with Arthur, hadn't realised the progress they had made. They were no more than fifty yards from the canopy.

Barry was throttling back. He was shouting, "D'you want me to take her in . . ?" Twenty yards to go . . . fifteen . . . ten . . . Suddenly there was desperate anxiety because they had been far longer than they had scheduled; could London hold the test area as it was? Would it remain sufficiently stable to let them through?

"Well done!" They hurriedly changed places. "Leave Arthur in the bottom; you balance it that side."

As they speeded up again, shot through into the Time Field, it began to collapse. It was different from going through the other way; the tow was tremendous, they were being dragged back.

The physical force was such that you didn't feel terror; it annihilated feeling. It took all you had to concentrate on hanging on – to will yourself from being torn in two.

Luke found himself shouting; not words he was aware of, but mere encouragement. Their faces were contorted.

*

Then it was over. With a final lurch and a flood of water, the dinghy made it. They were back in their own time with a calm sea and the *Artemis* hardly rolling and the beautiful, beautiful twentieth century; the not-so-calm face of the Captain on the bridge because he thought they had left it too late and couldn't understand why there were still three figures in the gemini dinghy – and the positively twitchy one of Davies on the casing. Luke had never thought before how beautiful their world was; but he decided then. He wouldn't leave it again willingly.

Ropes were out from the submarine and they were pulled in; seized by thankful hands and greeted by cheerful faces. It had been a time of tremendous anxiety for everyone. Dazed and deafened by their experience, Barry and Luke had to be helped back on board.

Arthur, returned from the dead, was brought up like a corpse on a makeshift pulley.

They put him into Luke's bunk. He was unconscious. He was washed and cleaned up and the doctor exclaimed over his battered body.

"What made him punish himself like this?"

"He was up against it," said Luke, so full of joy that he still didn't really believe it was Arthur lying there, torn and shredded. It had to be digested slowly.

"A lucky chap by the sound of it," the doctor said, filling a syringe. "Hold his arm for me, will you? No, more that way. Fine."

"Not lucky," said Luke, "clever and brimful of guts. Tumbled to something no one else did. There aren't many like this one."

"Must have had strong reasons for surviving," said the doctor cheerfully; he was a blood and guts man, embarrassed by this young man's obvious emotion. They put them in charge before they were out of the cradle these days; the strain on them was far too punishing.

"He had very strong reasons for surviving." Luke suddenly alarmed by Arthur's inert face said, "He'll be all right, won't he?"

"Soon have him on his feet again," said the doctor, bouncing and confident, "such as he's got left," he added.

When Arthur came round two days later, he didn't recognise any of them.

Chapter 10

October

A hot and oppressive day, with London overcast, gritty with the dust of a late Indian summer. As Luke, bound for the Institute, turned out of the Strand and into Kent Street it was like a cool hand to a fevered brow to see the Embankment and the river sliding past at the bottom. Propped between two more prosperous neighbours, the Institute was as shabby as ever. The pillars by the front door were now so chipped and cracked that in places they had gone through the plaster to their original stone. No money to spare for external coats of paint, Arthur had always said. Still they hardly needed a grant to polish the brass plate by the entrance; it was now so mildewed over that you were quite unaware that you were standing on the threshold of the *L'Institut pour la Promotion en Physique Européen*. The bell that had been broken when Luke first stood on the Institute steps three years before, still failed to work. He pushed open the front door and went in. Tom was in the hall.

"Should we go out?" he said. "Nice to get a breath of air by the river."

They walked east along the embankment towards the City.

Tom said, "I've got a proposition, Luke."

"That sounds familiar."

Tom said defensively, "Well, last time it worked out, didn't it?"

"That's a matter of opinion," Luke said heavily.

"From a scientific point of view, it was a hundred per cent success and well you know it," Tom said evenly.

"From a human point of view, it was a bloody awful mess."

"Only time will tell that."

Luke shrugged. "It doesn't seem on our side at the moment."

"You can't carry that on your back for ever."

"I don't see I've got any choice."

"Well, it's shared, isn't it?" said Tom, sounding angry. "And you can't go through your life a guilt-ridden martyr, you're not helping anyone by doing that. Certainly not Mary nor Arthur. And you know perfectly well, Luke, that but for your handling of the job and your damned cool courage, everything might have turned out a hell of a lot worse."

"Sorry, didn't mean to rile you," Luke said shortly. "I'm not fishing for compliments. You were absolutely right; they were a first-class team."

They walked along in silence, each with his own thoughts.

"It's only a month yet; no time at all and the treatment these days is pretty sophisticated . . . "

Luke thought privately that Tom was fooling no one, least of all himself. Treatment *was* sophisticated and Arthur, who had had the best, should have responded to it by now if he was going to.

"Yup." One thing the experiment had done and that was help to remove the barrier between himself and Tom; the last time Tom had made a proposition there had been a gulf between them that seemed impossible to span; but Tom no longer intimidated Luke in the same way; he now had the confidence to stand up for himself. He supposed you got it from carrying through a job.

"You're more aware of people than you used to be, Tom."

Tom sighed unexpectedly. "Perhaps it's circumstances." He didn't enlarge upon it although Luke, for a moment, thought he was going to. No one would ever get close to Tom; he had got as near as one ever would on the evening when he had told him of Arthur's disappearance; when just for a moment he had looked very young, crushed and utterly defeated.

"I'm not interested in people like you are," he said. "Oh I can assess their competence, their suitability for a job – you don't think I asked you to sit in on the experiment three years ago out of kindness of heart, do you? I had an eye on the main chance even then; I saw your potential. I'm a great opportunist you know. But I've come to the end of the road with the Institute, Luke. I realise

it more and more. I want to work in the abstract now; stick wholly
to theories. It isn't a new idea – I've been moving towards it for
some time."

"You want to go back to Cambridge?"

"Or over to America. R.G. at Batavia wants me to join him."

"Well, why not, you've the most colossal knowledge and
experience to offer."

"What's going to happen to the Institute if I go?" said Tom.

Luke looked at the river sliding down towards London docks; it
had been sliding down for ever; since well before the time of
Jonah; it would go on like this with any luck for aeons more,
unless the politicians and the scientists between them were
stupid enough to destroy everything.

"Oh no, Tom," he said. "Oh no. Don't ask me."

He didn't go back with Tom to Kent Street; he walked to
Liverpool Street to get his train for Cambridge. Followed the river
and then struck up north. He felt the need of time to think. And
after all if Arthur could cover upward of sixty miles in two days at
the height of an Israeli summer, what was a walk along London
pavements with stout soles on his shoes and the possibility of
stopping every half mile for liquid refreshment if he wanted it.

Only now did he realise how much he had been looking
forward to his doctorate, to getting back to his college – to
separate himself from the life of the horrific, hectic summer; to
return to live with people who knew nothing about submarines
and weren't interested in tachyons. So, like Tom, he could shut it
all off in a compartment of his mind and say – "Finished".

But nothing had resolved itself the next morning when he sat
on the window seat of his college room looking over Gonville
Court as Arthur had done three months before. The court,
refaced in the 18th century, had a pleasing classical simplicity; a
monastic quietness. In its one flower bed, below Luke's window,
late roses were still in bloom. And the grass in the centre was very
green. Patterned in squares by cross cutting, it had the precise
neatness of a chess board. Even now a gardener was tending its
perfection.

Peaceful and academic. The court was full of sunlight; a clock chimed the quarter with a medieval sound that went on vibrating on the warm air. Someone was playing the organ in the chapel, a rippling piece of Bach. The smell of soup wafted through the open window of the buttery.

Luke felt that it had been like this for centuries; was it his niche for life? It could be if he chose that way. Learned talk and academic honours; did it appeal to him? The tinkle of sherry glasses in Hall; candlelight; sonorous voices. All very civilised and a far cry from the shabby Institute and the rat race of London.

The problem seemed insoluble.

That evening he rang up Mary.

"When I came across you last December," said Mary, "I wanted my marriage gift-wrapped with a label 'Happiness Guaranteed'. Have you come to ask the same thing from me now? The top job at the Institute – *recommended: sure to bring satisfaction.*"

He had come up to London to see her; she had been to the hospital to visit Arthur that afternoon and had only just got back.

"If I take it," he said, "will I be betraying Arthur? After all that's happened to him, maybe it would be better if the Institute went to the wall . . ."

"That's a very emotive word 'betraying'," she said sharply (was she bitter, she had every right to be?). "If you don't want the job then say so, but don't make Arthur your excuse. You've got to make up your own mind about things like that, no one can do it for you. I had to over Arthur. If I remember you were appalled by the very thought of our wedding – that was fairly obvious."

He realised she was dead tired and thoroughly dispirited. He shouldn't have come. He must be out of his senses. She was absolutely right; it was his problem and his only. As if she hadn't enough problems of her own.

She lay back in an armchair and closed her eyes; they had dark rings under them. Her whole face had a strained, bloodless look.

"Sorry," he said wearily. "I'll make you a cup of tea – or

something stronger if you like. I won't raise the subject again. It's nothing to do with you."

He went out to the kitchen feeling ashamed of his crass stupidity and thoroughly at odds with himself. He filled the kettle and lit the stove and leaned against the sink waiting for the water to boil. He stared out of the window so entrenched in misery he didn't know whether to leave the flat there and then and never come back.

What a mess. What a bloody awful mess, as he had said to Tom. Arthur dead was hardly worse than Arthur cut off from them all – unable to communicate because he could remember nothing either about himself nor recognise any of them. And here was he crashing about making things a hundred times more difficult by loving the wrong person. At that moment the whole tangled problem of misguided intentions seemed to weigh so heavily on his shoulders that he could no longer support it.

"Luke ... Luke ... I'm sorry." She came padding into the kitchen having taken off her shoes. "It's difficult ... sometimes ... often ... when I come back home to the empty flat after seeing him ... to have any hope."

"No. My fault. I shouldn't have come."

"You must come," she spoke with great depth of feeling, "go on coming; you're a lifeline ... oh, in so many ways."

A lifeline. How ironic could things be? She must never know his feelings. Ever.

"How is he?"

"The same. They keep on saying anything may happen at any time. But it doesn't. It just needs something to trigger off his memory – if only he could identify himself, then they could probably help him. They say he'll never be a scientist again – well, I can face that – I just want him to be a *person*."

"He still doesn't know you ... ?"

She pressed her lips tightly together and shook her head, the tears welling up in her eyes. "Like a complete stranger. He doesn't *want* to know me – that's what hurts ... "

"It must come right. He wouldn't have survived all that he did, just to be ... well, like he is." He said it with fierce conviction.

"I keep clutching on to that," the tears were running down her face now, "and we've got him back, in body at least; that's better, surely so much better than we thought possible at one time . . . "

The kettle boiled and Luke made the tea and she gulped it down. How could she drink anything so hot?

"Don't cry," he said gently.

"There's some biscuits in that tin." She sat down behind the table and blew her nose. "Sorry."

"There's no need to be."

"If you want to follow Tom at the Institute, Arthur should encourage you, not deter you. The Institute was Arthur's life; he believed in it through and through and everything it did. Think how mad Simon made him by running it down. You must be positive if you believe in something. Can you remember him saying that? If you abandon the Institute, Luke, you'll be abandoning Arthur and all that he worked for. All that he's been through will have been in vain. Don't you understand?"

Arthur was still as powerful an influence in both their lives as if he had been standing there in the kitchen.

"But your heart *must* be in it," she said, "or it's no good. I think it is really or you couldn't have done what you did this summer."

"I think it is too. But just at the moment I'm so tired of making decisions. I want a rest from them. I seem to have been making them for ever . . . "

"The best decision you ever made," she said, "was to take Jonah back. If only I'd come with you."

"I wouldn't have taken you." He left no room for doubt. "And *you* brought Arthur through it all. He said so. Don't ever forget that."

"The best decision I ever made was to marry Arthur," she said. "We were meant together. I'm as sure of that as I was on our wedding day." Luke could feel her believing it in every fibre of her body. "For better, for worse . . . It wasn't invented lightly." She was calm again now.

"And Jonah?"

"Thank God for Jonah."

"Tom believes it was him."

"Of course it was. I should have known . . . those queer turns I had . . . "

"You thought they were Arthur?"

"They were Jonah. I was psyched in to Jonah."

"The Whale Hall . . . ?"

"And drawing lots with the spaghetti like the sailors drew lots when they threw Jonah out."

Luke thought musingly of the brine-soaked bundle of clothes in the torpedo room. A less impressive instrument of God it would be hard to find – and yet too late he had been struck by the strength of the man's face in the dinghy.

"There would be people glad to hear of how it happened," Mary said. "There's a body of sceptics who question the whole Book of Jonah because they say no one could survive in a fish for three days. We've given it a new significance."

"We'll steer clear of them if you don't mind," Luke said, "it's enough that Arthur realised the significance and got himself back to Haifa."

"Clever, clever Arthur. Trust him to see it," she said and opened the door of the fridge to get out a packet of frozen peas for their supper.

They stood around uncertainly wondering why they were there, picking up handfuls of potato crisps – that's all there was to eat, they were put out in filter dishes – and fingering their half pints of beer or glasses of Pimms as the case might be. They were all there, the team from the submarine and the team from London; the whole Institute in fact, asked by Tom to stay on that evening for a drink. It was such an unlikely invitation from unsociable Tom that they all managed to alter any plans they had for doing other things and stayed. Tom presumably knew the reason for the gathering and Luke thought he probably did too – though he hoped he might be wrong and steeled himself for an embarrassing moment.

The moment came sooner than he thought. Tom raised his voice and a bottle he was holding and bellowed, "Quiet everybody," and waited until the chatter dribbled to a standstill.

Then he said, "It may not come as a surprise to all of you – but to some it will – to hear that I'm going over to America in the near future." There was a murmur of surprise. "Permanently." The murmur became several loud exclamations. Tom had obviously kept his plans a pretty close secret up till now. Luke looking round thought Simon would be in the know, but more people than not seemed taken aback.

"I've given it a lot of thought," Tom said, twirling his glass and fixing it with an eye of concentration as if he was justifying himself to his drink rather than to his audience; he was not a natural speech maker. "It's not been an easy decision. But I've been at the Institute for nearly five years now and you have to progress in your work and thought. I'm going to join R.G. at Batavia. Anyway," – he abandoned his glass at last and looked around at them all – "no bad thing to have a change of man in charge – new brooms and all that – necessary once in a while if things aren't to get into a rut ... "

"We're not in a rut," said Dotty loudly.

"What's going to happen to the Institute then?" somebody shouted. And that was obviously in everyone's mind.

"I've given that a lot of thought too," Tom paused. Then he said. "Luke will be taking over. It hasn't been an easy decision for him either because as you know he's all set for a doctorate. He has the full support of the Board; you couldn't be in better hands. Need I say that he proved himself this summer ... "

He was drowned by everyone talking and shouting. Hands seized Luke and pushed him up onto a table; there was clapping and stamping and some idiot started 'For he's a jolly good fellow'. With creditable prep school humour they carried it through. Then there were cheers for Tom and Tom received his accolade.

"Speech! Luke!"

A strange thing happened to Luke. In that moment of spontaneous and genuine approval from his friends, it came home to him that the Institute was his. Before it had always meant Tom. For the person at the top moulded it; shaped it; did what he would.

He would make a success of it in a different way from Tom.

He looked round the shabby, crumbling common room; at the faded wallpaper and the sagging armchairs. Someone had lit a solitary candle under the only picture – an inappropriate portrait of Montgomery left by the previous owners. He looked at the cheerful, smiling faces; Nick who he liked more than anyone; dependable Kristof and Graham; Dotty and Sheila and Becky, pillars of strength on the *Artemis*. Alan Blériot who he had known the longest, who had given him his first interview; and yes, even ghastly Barry Lambert was part of *his* set up.

Last of all he looked at Tom and saw Tom no longer as someone above him but as an equal – outstanding in calibre yes, but a challenge to be met. Tom had made the Institute what it was and its achievements were tremendous. But he could see it developing along different lines – he could see potential that Tom had never explored. He caught Tom's eye and Tom raised his glass and nodded and Luke felt that he knew by instinct that their roles had already changed.

"The first thing I shall do," he said, "is to get hold of some Brasso and clean the plate by the front door!"

An enormous feeling of excitement took hold of him. He began to speak with confidence and authority. He told them that they had made amazing discoveries in the past but that the past was over and done with; that he believed very strongly that the *future* now was where they must concentrate their thought.

He hoped, he said, they would stay with the Institute, every one of them – but if they had any doubts about the importance of the work there, then they had no place. He felt no compunction in saying this; he did not want the kind of situation that Tom had had to cope with with Simon; he wanted to be free to concentrate his energies on his scientific goals. Simon, himself, had told Luke he was going on to another job and Luke was glad.

Lastly he spoke of Arthur. Arthur who was as much part of the Institute as he had ever been – and always would be. Both he and Mary needed their support; he hoped every person standing in that room would give it unstintingly . . .

After three more weeks of unsuccessful treatment Arthur came home to the flat. He was like a lost soul. He could settle to nothing; he just seemed to want to sit and stare into space. And yet, thought Luke, he still has his dignity. He couldn't have borne it if Arthur had lost that. He wondered how long Mary could carry on looking after him in the selfless way she did. They tried continually to stimulate him – to interest him in what they were doing even if they were only sweeping the floor. But he showed no interest in anything.

Luke called in when he could. At least he had the distraction of his work; Mary had no respite.

"Do you know me?" he said to Arthur.

"No."

"You don't know I'm Luke?"

"No."

"But you know Mary?"

"No."

Luke despaired.

Anniversary

It was now summer again, a year since plans were first made for the Humboldt Effect.

Why did they badger him?
He wanted peace.
He had all he needed. Food. Drink.
He just wanted to sit. And think. And look. At nothing in particular.
Fluid. That's what he thought about. Fluid.
Fluid had no hardness; a soft surface that yielded to the mind. No pain. No harassment.
Who was the girl? He began to notice her scent. He hadn't noticed her scent before. The smell of her scent disturbed him. Stirred something. He didn't know what. Upset his peace. Nagged at his mind.
He didn't want nagging. He wanted peace.
He couldn't solve the puzzle of her scent.
So he would push her away.
So he could sit and look and not be upset.

"He's worse," she said in despair. "He's getting to hate me. He's pushing me away. He never did that before."

"There must be some way of getting through to him," said a frantic Luke, pacing up and down.

"I saw a programme on the television," said Nick Baines. "A boy brought out of a coma by having his teddy bear put beside him. The familiar feel of it stirred his subconscious."

But Mary had taken him home to the north. They had tried every connection with his childhood that they could.

"What would be the worst moment of all after he was swept off the *Artemis*?" said Luke.

Nick thought the journey alone through Israel when he was up against time and not knowing if he was on the right track.

Alan said the moment when he knew he was abandoned.

When would that be? Luke urgently wanted to know.

When the Time Field changed, they hazarded a guess. When the submarine disappeared.

Mary and Luke took Arthur to the Whale Hall at the Museum.

They chose a wet and windy day, late in the afternoon when the Museum was closed to the public. They had made the necessary arrangements. Arthur went with them, unwillingly, without interest.

The rain was drumming on the glass roof; Mary turned off the lights. They took Arthur up to the balcony over the whale. They left him standing there; then went away.

"We're going," said Luke roughly. "Leaving you."

"We're leaving you," Mary knew she had to carry it through; she hoped she had the strength to do it.

They went down the stairs into the hall below. They couldn't see Arthur clearly in the gloom, just his figure drooping over the balcony. They had a tape and a flashlight to re-enact the storm and they set the plan in motion.

"Jonah," Luke called out; he had to shout loudly above the noise of the tape. "*Jonah. Jonah. Jonah.*" It echoed weirdly. Despite herself, Mary found she was shaking. The whale was a great dark menacing shadow above them. Sea sounds broke around them.

Every moment that Arthur failed to react lasted an hour.

"Leaving you ... leaving you ... you ... oo."

Slowly, unbelievably slowly, Arthur straightened up. They felt rather than saw at that distance the tension in his body. Suddenly he gave a cry; the despair in it tore them apart.

"No. No. No not that."

Prepared as they were, when he shouted it made them both jump. Luke put a hand on Mary, "Wait!" But she had already

gone to him.
"We're here, Arthur. Arthur!"
Arthur had remembered.

They took him home in a taxi. He was like a man drugged; like someone emerging from a heavy sleep; totally disorientated, afraid. But for the first time for seven months, he was aware.
"There's hope," Mary said. "Oh Luke, there's hope, isn't there?"
When Luke left them at the flat, Arthur was holding on to Mary as if he would never let her go again.
Luke went back to the Institute alone.